WE HAVE TILL DAWN

CARA DEE

www.caradeewrites.com

We Have till Dawn

Copyright © 2020 by Cara Dee
All rights reserved

Edited by Silently Correcting Your Grammar, LLC.
Formatted by Eliza Rae Services.

DEDICATION

To NY bagels and guitar players.

CHAPTER 1

Nicky Fender

"Let me get this straight," I said, scanning the document. "The wife is the client? I mean, she's the one setting her husband up with a male escort?"

"Correct." Tina sat back as our server approached with dinner. "Well, her fiancé."

I hummed and kept my mouth shut until we were alone again. Fuck, the pizza looked good. Of course, meeting with Tina meant it had to be some fancy pizza. She wouldn't be caught dead with a regular slice. She wouldn't be caught dead in Brooklyn either, which was why I'd met up with her in Manhattan at some swanky Italian place. But hey, she was buying.

"I'm waiting for the reason for why I'd agree," I admitted bluntly. I hadn't whored out my sweet ass in two years, and I was doing much better now. I worked three jobs for very little pay, I lived with my big brother, and I had practically no time for any hobbies. What's not to love?

I'd thought about going back to Tina for some time, but whenever I considered it, there was this rock in the pit of my stomach that no amount of money could crush.

"I wanted you to see the requirements first," she replied.

Well, there were a lot of them. I hadn't gone through the entire list yet. After placing the document next to my plate, I cut into my fancy pizza and continued reading the list. There was plenty on hygiene, but nothing that went beyond what I was used to. I was to be blindfolded the whole time? All right... I'd never see the client's face—or the client's fiancé—which wasn't necessarily a bad thing.

"I get the impression from the client that the man wants to explore something before he agrees to marry her," Tina revealed. I'd heard of weirder dynamics. "She hinted that it would be a one-time arrangement, and she placed emphasis on following instructions that seem to cover every inch of your body."

Lovely.

"That's a lot of exploring," I pointed out. "He wants to meet with me four nights a week for two months."

Tina lifted a shoulder in a slight shrug and sipped her wine.

More specifically, I had to be available for him between the hours of ten PM and six AM on Tuesdays, Wednesdays, Thursdays, and Saturdays.

I scratched my ear.

The pay better be out of this world, 'cause I would have to quit at both Applebee's and Starbucks. Not that I'd mourn those shifts, but I'd been at Applebee's long enough to possibly make assistant manager when the current one quit next month. She was having a baby and moving to Jersey.

I stuck a piece of pizza into my mouth and eyed the requirements for safety, at which I almost choked on a pepperoni slice.

"How loaded is this couple?" I asked through a cough. The man demanded exclusivity, meaning I wasn't allowed to be sexually active with anyone else for the duration of our arrangement. And that cost a fucking mint.

"Read on..." Tina smirked wryly.

I furrowed my brow—then spotted one of my few hard limits. I shook my head and wiped my mouth with my napkin. "No fucking way. Tina, you—no. Fuck this."

I didn't mess around without protection. Not a chance in hell.

"This is why I asked you, Nicky," she told me patiently. "Considering your stance on protection and your sad little Facebook statuses on how single you are—" she ignored my glare "—not to mention that you're not the type of guy who walks around with a string of hookups, I can count on you passing a screening with flying colors *and* taking on someone who wants exclusivity. You're my only candidate."

"Candidate to say no," I retorted.

Tina adopted a smug expression and reached down to dig something out of her purse. "There's a reason I wanted to save the perks for last," she said. "Okay, so you know the requirements. An exclusive arrangement for both parties—during which you're sexually active only with each other—four nights a week for two months. You won't see him. He won't violate your limits—"

"Going unprotected *is* a limit, Tina," I grated. Fuck, I was getting pissed. Part of me had carried foolish hope that this would be such a golden case that I'd jump on the opportunity and earn some good dough before the rock in my stomach returned.

"And when you're an escort dealing with multiple clients a

week, nothing else would make sense," she answered, extending another document to me. "I wouldn't even try to approach my other sex workers with this, Nicky. You're the exception only because you quit the field."

"Hmpf." I cast a disgruntled look her way before I lowered my gaze to the piece of paper.

Ahem.

Holy fuck.

Three grand a week—minus Tina's finder's fee of ten percent—plus living arrangements. There would be a furnished studio in my name, so to speak, rent and utilities paid for by the client. Corner of West 39th and Ninth Avenue—not a shabby address at all. One of my best friends lived in the Garment District. Adjacent to Hell's Kitchen, where another friend lived.

A Manhattan address and $3,000 a week for two months.

A guy could do worse.

I shifted in my seat and cleared my throat. "Is there, uh, any way to ensure safety by making sure the guy gets tested too?"

"Of course, Nicky." The compassion in Tina's crystal-blue eyes reminded me of the fact that she ran an ethical business based on choice and vetting. She didn't headhunt sex workers; they had to come to her, and they—*we*—had to go through a selection process before she could, in good conscience, give us work.

Today I was an exception for her, and my answer would be an exception too.

It was with a good goddamn feeling that I walked into our favorite happy hour spot in Hell's Kitchen the next day, where my two closest friends were waiting at the bar. The place was packed as usual.

"Guess who just temporarily moved to Manhattan?" I hollered over the music and widened my arms.

Chris lifted his brows, and Ruby's mouth popped open in shock.

At long fucking last, I wouldn't have to blow them off for a while because I couldn't pay for my own drinks. Unlike my Armani-rocking buddy Chris, I hadn't been able to afford to go to college, much less a prestigious one like Yale. Today, he worked on Wall Street, and he'd made partner at his firm before he turned thirty-five two years ago. And unlike Ruby, I wasn't destined for a life in modeling. With her Peruvian and Nigerian ancestry, she'd spent approximately three weeks at Pratt before a modeling agency had snatched her up. These days, she walked the runways in Milan, London, and Paris, and she was making bank to the point where she'd just become a Manhattan homeowner. She'd legit bought her place here in Hell's Kitchen.

"Wait." She slid off her barstool and narrowed her eyes at me. "You had lunch with Tina yesterday."

So she'd seen my Instagram post. "Guilty as charged." I gave the bartender a nod and a two-finger wave. "It's only a two-month stint." I paused to order a beer and two more of whatever Chris and Ruby were drinking. Then I turned back to Ruby. "Three thousand bucks a week and my own studio, and some faceless millionaire will stop by every now and then to explore his sexuality. I think I can deal." I smirked.

"Just be careful, buddy." Chris took a swig of his new drink, and I snatched up my beer and handed over my credit card to the bartender.

"I don't think I'll have anything to worry about," I replied. "There was a whole section in the contract about letting him set the pace, and it was written in a way that makes me believe he's anxious or something. I don't fucking know." I shrugged and took a sip of my beer. "Like I said, it's two months. Then I'll be able to go into business with Anthony."

My brother ran a successful music academy out in Park Slope, and he'd been trying to scrape together the money to expand for years. He wanted me with him, and I wanted the same, but he also knew I'd turn him down if he offered a partnership without my bringing any green to the table. But now, I'd get my shot at actually getting somewhere.

I'd landed the golden opportunity I'd hoped for.

Ruby still had concern brimming in her eyes, probably because I'd told her about the rock I'd had in my stomach before I quit being a sex worker last time. This was different, though. I wholeheartedly believed it.

"Quit worryin', mami." I draped an arm around her shoulders and kissed her temple. "I'm relieved. I feel good about my decision."

She pursed her glossy lips and eyed me critically, but I could sense her thawing. She snaked an arm around my middle, then sighed and mustered a smile. "You're the baby in our group, you know that. It's my job to worry."

She was, like, three years older than me, not three decades. She just turned thirty the other week.

"Fine," she conceded eventually. "If you're happy, I'm happy, and you deserve to be celebrated."

I smacked another kiss to her cheek before I slid onto the middle stool. I was definitely in the mood for some celebrating.

Chris clapped me on my back and said the rest of the drinks were on him tonight.

"I knew it was true. Once you're flush with cash, everything's free." I reached for a bowl of bar nuts and grabbed a handful.

"Gross, Nicky," Ruby chided.

I ate them noisily, much to her displeasure.

"I need older friends," Chris muttered into his glass.

"You wouldn't dare abandon us," I told him.

"Please," Ruby snorted. "You'd get bored in a second."

That was what was funny about Chris. In our little group of friends, he was the mellow, mature guy. Around his work buddies—the older ones, not the young weekend warriors who did more coke than Tony Montana—he was restless and reckless.

The only time Ruby and I saw that other side of him was when I had a gig. My brother and I, along with two of his friends, had a band together on and off, and Chris jumped in as our bass player when Marco was a no-show. And with six kids, that happened frequently.

It was how I'd met Chris. He'd been at one of our shows, and when Marco had to split, I'd jokingly asked the crowd if anyone played bass. A hammered Chris had put his fist into the air and volunteered. Marco hadn't dared to put up a fight about whether he'd let Chris borrow his instrument.

It was a great memory of mine, even though our gig had sucked. Chris still had plenty of talent.

We left the bar right around the same time as the sun was glowing red and slowly dipping between two skyscrapers.

I had a good buzz going on and hoped we'd try that new place near Ruby's building.

"When do you get your keys?" Chris asked, patting his pockets to make sure he had his wallet. Or phone. Or both.

"Already got them," I replied and shrugged on my jacket. Fall was here. Chris liked to point out that I should get a "grown man" jacket, presumably one like his countless different coats, blazers, and windbreakers. But there was nothing wrong with my army jacket; I wore it in the winter too, just with a hoodie underneath. "Anthony's helping me move some shit over to the studio tomorrow night."

I was only bringing two or three duffels, my keyboard, and a guitar, but I couldn't lug it all on the subway unless I wanted to go back and forth all day. My brother had a car, so that helped.

When I caught Ruby yawning, I mock-gasped and pointed at her. "What the fuck?"

She groaned and threw an arm around me. "I'm sorry, but I'm so fucking tired. I've been up since four."

I cast a downward glance at her feet. No wonder she was suddenly taller than me. She was wearing six-inch heels. I hadn't noticed before.

"I'm getting you an Irish coffee at the next place," I told her. She winced.

"*Ruby.*" I couldn't believe it. She was calling it a night. I could feel it.

"I'm tired too," Chris admitted. "I gotta be up at six tomorrow for a meeting."

It was just barely dinnertime!

"I'm disappointed in both'a youse." I shook my head and stepped closer to the curb.

We went back and forth for a while; Ruby promised to make it up to me when we met up for breakfast on Saturday after my first session with my mystery client, and it made me feel bad. She wanted to make sure I'd be okay, and I was giving her shit, knowing full well that she worked insane hours. So, in the end, Chris and I stayed on the sidewalk after hugging Ruby good-night, and we waited until she'd disappeared into her building farther up the street.

I wasn't ready to head home to Brooklyn. I had a key to a new apartment that would be mine for the next two months, and I had someone to share a cab with me over to the Garment District.

"What's good to eat in your neighborhood?" I asked as we got into a cab.

Chris blew out a breath and patted his flat stomach. "I've had too much Arby's."

I liked Arby's.

"There's plenty along Ninth," he went on. "Some good sushi and Italian." He paused. "The bagel vendor on the corner across from the 7-Eleven is probably the best in Manhattan."

Good to know. There weren't many good bars in his area, so we didn't meet up there often.

I peered out the window as the last light left the horizon between the buildings. It was the time of day I liked the most, because it was when my New York City woke up. I loved all of it. The city lights, the noise, the energy, the people minding their own business.

If I could be paid to people watch, it would've been the career of my dreams.

Twenty minutes later, I had an Arby's bag in one hand and my new key in the other.

I took the elevator up to the twenty-seventh floor and felt weirdly nervous. When Tina had given me the key earlier, it hadn't felt real yet. It hadn't even felt real when I'd gone in for a quick STI screening where Tina had sent me so many times before. But now, shit, I was getting back to it. Temporarily or not, I'd be a sex worker once more.

When I'd first started working for Tina, I'd actually loved it. I'd seen it as a well-paid adventure. Given the clientele that could afford browsing her, uh, menu, I'd dined with shy tech millionaires, fucked politicians, and received lavish gifts from closeted CEOs. I'd seen what New York had to offer from the most expensive hotel suites. Those who met with escorts to live out their secret fantasies and be themselves were usually the nicest. To them, we were escapes. But I'd also been with clients who treated us like objects. It was part of the job. There was no denying that.

Ultimately, though, what'd caused this dark void within me was the sense of being fleeting in someone's life. To always exist on the fringes of another person's life took a toll. According to my pop, it was something I'd gotten from my mother. She'd worn her heart on her sleeve when she was alive. I was similar. I loved people. I loved to help. It was why I worked with children at my brother's academy. It was the most rewarding job I'd had.

Stepping out of the elevator, I glanced left then right. Eight apartments on each floor.

Three thousand dollars a week... All cash. In two months, I should be able to walk up to my brother and hand over almost twenty grand and make myself a partner in his business.

Two months. I could do this. I *wanted* to do this.

Apartment 2704 was mine. I turned the key in the lock and opened the door, and it was kinda fucking impossible to fight a grin. There was no entryway to speak of, and the place was small, but I loved it. It was one open space. Bathroom straight ahead, an alcove next to it just big enough for the bed and two nightstands that were already there, kitchen area to my left, closet behind the door, a small table with two chairs by the kitchen window.

The biggest window was six or so feet to the right, in the alcove, and I walked over to it with my Arby's bag and dug out my brisket sandwich.

Fuck me, this could work. Amazing view of the best city in the world. The buildings glittered in the night. This one had thirty stories in total, and I knew there was a terrace on the roof. I'd go up there tomorrow night when I had my guitar here.

I took a bite of my sandwich and glanced down at the tiny cars on the street.

Then I took a little tour of my new home and decided there was no reason for me to return to Brooklyn tonight. There was fresh linen on the bed, shower products and toiletries in the bathroom, and even some water, fruit, and snacks in the kitchen.

Exposed brick walls painted white, state-of-the-art kitchen appliances, the softest towels, tiny spotlights under the four kitchen cupboards... There was no TV, but I spotted an iPad on one of the nightstands. Was this some fucking hotel? No pun intended.

There was a note on the table, so I sat down with my Arby's bag and pulled out my soda and fries too. No "dear guest" or "esteemed whore" or anything; it went straight to the Wi-Fi password and some instructions.

Before each meeting, all lights had to be turned off, and the blackout curtains—whoa, blackout curtains? I snapped my gaze to the windows, and wouldja look at that. I'd missed those before. Okay, I had to shut them before the mystery man arrived, and I had to put on the sleep mask that was located in the nightstand drawer.

I didn't know if I was insulted by the instructions on how I should shower before the meetings too. Did the client think I was some filthy pig?

Maybe he was a germophobe.

All communication would go through the iPad, and there was a list of information I was supposed to send him. *"No chitchat, please."* Jeez. Throwing some fries into my mouth, I walked over to the tablet and swiped on the screen. A test message had been sent already.

I sent him a couple messages with the details he'd requested. And no chitchat.

No allergies, I prefer oil-based lube or coconut oil, minimal scarring (I was a clumsy kid), no piercings, yes to tattoos—my right shoulder and down my arm.

Five foot ten, green eyes, brown hair, I'm 27, nonsmoker, yes to alcohol every now and then, no mental (or otherwise) disabilities, no trauma in the past, no triggers. I'm not on any medications, and my test results will be ready on Monday.

I cocked my head as the "Read" sign popped up at the bottom. Would he respond? Or was his fiancée handling this too? Would *she* respond? I returned to the table to finish my food, and I kept staring, kept waiting, until I realized that was it. No chitchat. He would sit on all the information and give nothing in return.

I huffed and took a swig of my soda.

Screw this, I had the right to ask for something too.

After finishing the last of my sandwich, I wiped the grease off my fingers and then typed in a message.

Your turn.

The standard "Delivered" never showed; it went to "Read" immediately, making me wonder if someone still had his messages open.

That someone started typing, and it tightened my stomach a bit.

Is Nick your real name?

Not what I expected. I wanted answers, dammit. I wanted at least a name and maybe...fuck if I knew, some personal info that gave me a clearer image of him. Right now, he was just a blob.

Nick was the name Tina used for my clients. Most sex workers I'd known went by fake names, and technically, I did too, 'cause it was assumed my real name was Nicholas when it was Nicola. But no one called me that.

I fired off a quick response.

It's a version of my name. Some details about you wouldn't hurt.

I set down the tablet and threw more fries into my mouth. He was typing, and time would tell if he would give me something or not. Part of me wanted to ask Tina, but that'd be a waste. No matter how little intel a client gave her, she always got enough to figure out who someone was, and she kept it to herself.

Just as I started chewing on the last of my fries, a rather lengthy text popped up.

My name is Gideon. I'm 44 years old, 6'4", brown eyes, brown hair, and I don't have any tattoos or piercings. I have Asperger's and need to stay in control for this arrangement, so please let me set the pace. I will see you on Saturday night. Expect my instructions for the evening one hour before my arrival. That's enough chitchat. Good night.

I raked my teeth along my bottom lip and read the message a couple more times. I had to admit I was intrigued. At my brother's music academy, I sometimes came across an autistic student, and their way of thinking fascinated me. They often had a whole other world to show you; you just needed to tap into their language.

Gideon. All right, I was ready.

CHAPTER 2

"You're not gonna tell Pop and Nonna about this, are you?" I lifted my T-shirt and wiped my forehead.

"Tell 'em what, that you're leaving Brooklyn or that you're turning tricks?"

I shot my brother a bitchy look, to which he laughed.

"Fuck no, I'm not telling them about a temporary move," he chuckled.

Good. Whenever something major was happening, we told our family as little as possible. Nonna was a drama queen, and Pop hated change. Their entire world existed across the East River in the same neighborhood where they'd always lived. I remembered when Anthony moved ten minutes away and Nonna thought he was gonna forget about her.

We'd figured out the best way to keep her calm was to continue traditions from our childhoods. For instance, I still met up with Nonna once a week at Sahadi's, not really for the shopping but for the company and so she could see that I was alive and well.

She had two gay grandsons and still believed we faced dangers on every street corner, even though Anthony had been out since he was like thirteen, approximately...many years ago... Fuck, I had to do math here. He was forty-two. He'd been out a long time, and yet Nonna never stopped worrying.

She was also a violent, scrappy little lady. She could wrap her fingers around a wooden spoon and go, "If you ever get bullied for the gay thing, I'll mess a fucker right up." Then she'd do the Sign of the Cross and send a quick apology to God for cursing.

The gay thing.

Never mind that my brother was six-two and had trained in kickboxing since he was ten; our five-foot-nothing little grandmother was gonna take care of any bullies. With a wooden spoon.

"Let's order pizza." There wasn't much else to do. I'd set up my keyboard in the bedroom window, my clothes were stowed away in the closet, my guitar was under the bed, and I'd left some personal items in the nightstand drawer, in the bathroom, and on the kitchen counter. Because I wasn't moving to Manhattan without my sundae glassware and collection of sauces and maraschino cherries.

"Do they have that here?" Anthony asked with a straight face.

I snorted and sat down at the table with my phone. "Ray's delivers. Does that work for your highness?"

My family hated Manhattan, including Anthony, which made no sense. We were the Italian-Irish Americans who'd grown up in a Latin neighborhood in Williamsburg, the part that hadn't been taken over by rich hipsters and artists. In short, we'd lived and breathed old-school culture and Catholicism our entire lives, and Anthony's first words as a toddler had been, "I'm gonna leave this place one day." Probably in Spanish. At least, according to Pop, and grumpy old men never exaggerated. But apparently, my brother's idea of leaving was to move ten minutes south to Park Slope. Granted, Park Slope had a better LGBTQ community, not to mention house prices that made any queen gasp dramatically.

Anthony was dating one of those.

While I ordered us a large pie to share, he grabbed two beers from the fridge.

Speaking of Anthony's queen... "Don't tell Shawn I'm working for Tina again," I said.

I wouldn't trust that guy to keep it to himself.

"Give me some credit," Anthony replied and cocked a brow. "Don't mistake my silence for approval, though."

I wasn't. I knew he didn't like it.

"I can handle your reluctant support a lot better than his catty digs," I said. "Speaking of, when are you breaking up with him?"

He sighed heavily and patted his pockets, presumably for his smokes, but he knew he couldn't smoke here. "I thought we could skip that topic today."

Fine, but I'd keep bringing it up. He and Shawn didn't make sense. My brother was a mellow, rough-around-the-edges, sweet, jeans-and-T-shirt type of guy with a passion for music, wood-working, Sunday dinners with our family, and working with kids. Shawn was an egotistical diva who took advantage of the fact that Anthony was lonely.

My brother deserved better.

"I'll try again soon," I assured. "Maybe at dinner on Sunday."

"Can't wait." He yawned and checked his phone. "Damn, it's past ten already."

Shit, really?

"You could take your slices to go," I suggested, knowing he had work early. On Saturdays, he was in his workshop at the ass-crack of dawn to repair and sometimes build instruments. It was his side gig.

"I probably should." He scrubbed a hand along his jaw and glanced over his shoulder. "It's one hell of a view you got, though."

I followed his gaze and looked out the window. "Yeah, it's somethin'." And tomorrow I'd block it out before Gideon arrived. Which reminded me... "Don't you have a teenage student who's autistic?"

I taught children of all ages at Anthony's place, and it was always with the goal of them learning to play instruments. If they had a diagnosis, they were on the high-functioning sides of whatever spectrum.

Whereas Anthony had actually gone to college and used his degree in psychology to combine music with therapy. Or rather, music *was* a type of therapy, especially for children and teenagers with autism who found rhythm soothing.

"I have a few." He lifted his brows a bit, maybe confused by the random topic change.

I went with the truth. "The client I'm seeing tomorrow is autistic, so I was wondering if you had any general advice."

He shook his head slowly and rested his forearms on the table. "Nothing beyond what you already know. Ask before assuming, pay attention to his body language, and don't initiate touch until he says it's okay."

A little bit of a problem there, considering I'd be blindfolded.

"How old is he?" Anthony asked.

"Forty-four," I replied. "He said he's got Asperger's, but I thought you told me they stopped diagnosing that one."

"It's probably an older diagnosis, then." He shrugged a little. "As long as you communicate properly, I'm sure you'll be fine."

And what if what I called communicating, Gideon called chitchat?

Oh, whatever. Time would tell. It wasn't my first rodeo, and I was good at reading people. Once upon a time, I'd been one of Tina's most popular escorts. I was quick on my feet, and that helped.

By eight thirty the following evening, I was clean as a whistle and sitting on the edge of the bed, eating Chinese food naked. Asshole waxed, area around my cock trimmed, balls and face shaved. I was as cute as I was hot. Though, I doubted Gideon would take full advantage tonight since we weren't getting the test results until Monday. But he was free to feel me up and explore good and proper.

I felt a sense of melancholy that I didn't understand, but it could be the song playing on my laptop on the kitchen table. Anthony had sent me the live recording from our last gig, and the cover we'd played, "Cages," was special to me. It wasn't so much the lyrics as it was the two of us playing together. Up onstage was where I loved working with my brother the most.

I stuck some noodles into my mouth and caught sight of my reflection in the window as Anthony's voice filled the air. He sang as if he'd been through all the circles of hell and come back to tell the world about it. It was both strong and raspy. A voice with a force to be reckoned with. Mine was gentler and lower, and I couldn't hit the highest notes that he did with ease.

My reflection blended in with the city lights and the silhouettes of the skyscrapers, and I cocked my head and drew my hand through my hair. I was due for a cut soon, but I usually waited until Anthony pointed it out. Because he'd share some story of how I'd inherited our mother's hair. It was wavier. Anthony would weave his fingers through it sometimes and smile a little in a way that told me he was thinking of her.

Then he'd say, "Time for a cut, bambino."

These two months couldn't go by fast enough. As much as I was loving living in my own apartment in Manhattan, my dream was to go into business with Anthony. With $20,000, we could expand. We could build the recording studio we had the equipment but no space for, we could hire another teacher and start more classes...

Still no rock in the pit of my stomach.

I was sure it had to do with my finally having a fucking plan.

The iPad lit up next to me, and I swallowed the food in my mouth and opened the message from Gideon.

Arriving at ten. This is a reminder to close the curtains and put on the sleep mask. Instructions for the evening: lie on your back on the bed, without any clothes or covers, and don't make a sound or movement unless I ask you a direct question or something is wrong. Please confirm.

The melancholy took a hike and was replaced by a familiar thrill I hadn't felt since I first began working for Tina.

There was a possibility I would actually find this exciting.

I responded after sticking half an egg roll into my mouth.

Understood. Curtains closed, mask on, no covers, no sound, no movement.

Here we go.

He hadn't mentioned anything about the light, so I left the one on the nightstand on, because I didn't think Gideon would arrive with night-vision goggles. Then I folded down the duvet on the bed and took my spot in the middle. The sleep mask sat snugly and didn't allow for any peeking; I couldn't even see anything along the edges.

Deep breaths.

I relaxed against the mattress and tried to push away those invasive, obsessive thoughts that tended to creep in before I met a new client. The panicky ones that yelled that Gideon could be a serial killer or kidnapper. That kind of shit.

Deep breaths.

I adjusted my pillows and suppressed a shiver. It wasn't warm enough in the apartment to walk around naked forever.

Any minute now.

Deep breaths.

The sound of a key turning in the lock sent my pulse through the roof. This was it. He was here. The door opened and closed, and the lock was twisted again. Madonn', it was difficult to lie still, knowing he was probably watching me.

At the same time, it was thrilling. I wasn't bad to look at.

He walked closer. The sound was familiar; he wore dress shoes, not sneakers or anything like it. Dress shoes against wooden floors. Then he stopped, and a chair was pulled out. There was some fabric rustling. It was insane how heightened my senses became when I couldn't use my eyes.

I had to remind myself to breathe calmly.

Another few steps closer brought him to the alcove, and I didn't know what to expect, but I tensed up for a second when the bed dipped and he sat down on the edge next to me. The anticipation was going to fucking kill me. Was he a rough kind of man? Was he gentle? Cautious? Nervous? I could barely remember my own exploring of guys. Since Anthony was fifteen years older than me, he'd been out for as long as I'd been alive, and it'd been normalized in our home. I just knew one day that I was into men, and there'd been no stigma. It hadn't felt weird to explore, no more than what most went through. Teenage nerves, but never fear. I'd been lucky.

If Gideon was using a sex worker at the age of forty-four to explore, something told me he didn't have the easy background that I did, sexuality-wise.

He lowered his hand carefully onto my thigh, and as soon as I felt his fingers trembling, my own nerves took a hike.

If I concentrated hard, I could hear his unsteady breathing.

Instinct told me to help him, to reassure him, to guide him, but that would go against the rules, and I had no idea how he'd react. Two months was quite a while; it was probably better to be patient and win his trust.

He stroked my thigh slowly, down to my knee, then up until his fingertips teased my hip. "You're incredibly beautiful."

Fuck me, so was his voice. He'd spoken too quietly, but there was no mistaking a solid, warm, masculine voice.

I exhaled as he slid his hand across my abs.

I wasn't sure anyone had ever called me beautiful. Hot, sexy, handsome, attractive, cute—never beautiful. The word felt different. It didn't settle within me like most compliments did.

The scent of his cologne reached me when his hand shifted up to my chest, and it was as mouthwatering as the best kind of porn. It matched his voice, however that was possible.

Not giving a fuck about how shallow it made me, I hoped he didn't tell me to lose the mask, because there was no way his appearance would live up to the sound of him and his scent.

He took his time touching me, and I had to admit it felt hella amazing. Foreplay and sensuality were lost arts. I couldn't even remember the last time I'd been with someone who wasn't impatient in bed.

He drew in a breath and cautiously dipped his hand between my legs.

I felt my jaw tick with tension, because I had to struggle to remain still. The fucker was getting to me. It was hot. And I hadn't gotten laid in ages.

For each minute that went by, he became more at ease with touching me. I hoped he read my body and knew he was turning me on. There was no hiding the goose bumps or the shivers. Or the fact that my cock was getting harder.

Just when I thought it couldn't get more difficult to keep still and quiet, two sounds proved me wrong. Gideon was unbuckling his belt using only one hand, and that was followed by a zipper being pulled down.

Did he not want me to please him? He was the one paying me. I could be on my knees with his cock down my throat right now.

He withdrew his hand and rose from the bed. The rustling of fabric was enough to let me know he was shedding his clothes, and I wondered if he was gonna speak again anytime soon. Did he even have a plan? If I wasn't mistaken, autistic people liked planning ahead.

I had to calm the fuck down and just go with the flow. It wasn't usually a problem for me.

Gideon joined me in bed again, and this time, he was coming back for more. He climbed over me and extended my arm to, um...what was he—oh. All right. My arm became his pillow as his head landed on my shoulder. Did he wanna cuddle? I was freaking lost. Even though I'd actually had plenty of clients who were starved for affection and wanted something like this rather than a quick release. I felt for all of them.

"I'm tired," he murmured, brushing his fingers over my chest. "I'm so tired."

He wasn't talking about physical exhaustion from a long day

at work. I heard it in his tone. It was something that ran way deeper, and I knew it was only a matter of seconds before I broke the rules, because that shit, that sort of pain, always tugged at me.

I wanted to say something.

I had to.

"You said I could speak if something was wrong." The words left me in a rush, and it was a fucking relief.

Gideon stiffened next to me. "What's wrong?"

"I'd like to hold you, unless it would make you uncomfortable."

He didn't answer right away, nor did he relax. He swallowed hard. His fingers had stopped drawing aimless patterns on my chest, and it was like lying next to a log. One that smelled amazing. His body was warm and solid.

He'd shaved before coming here. The way his cheek and jaw felt against my shoulder made it clear.

"Okay," he answered eventually. There was enough wariness in his voice for me to take things slowly and be prepared for anything.

"I'll make it comfortable for us," I promised. I carefully drew back my arm and told him I was just going to pull the duvet over us. He said nothing in response, so I hoped that was a silent agreement.

Once I was back, I slipped my arm underneath his pillow. "Rest your head here. I've got you."

With him being significantly taller than me, I shifted as high on my own pillow as I could, then scooted closer to him and snaked my free arm around his middle. His body heat and finally being under the covers made me shudder in contentment.

The man was pretty fit. Drawing my fingers up and down his back made me wanna see him. A little. His body, at least.

He shivered violently as I scratched him along his spine.

Slowly but surely, he relaxed in my embrace and snuck one leg between mine.

"It's nice, innit?"

"Yes, but it wasn't my plan," he replied.

How far could I push it? Would he feel comfortable enough to tell me to pipe down if I talked too much? Or asked too much?

I decided to save the questions.

"We have time." I pressed my lips to his hair—his soft fucking hair. Jesus Christ. "You set the pace. If you wanna rest, we'll rest. If you want more, we'll do more."

He let out a long breath and nodded once. "Okay."

Maybe I was the one who was starved for affection.

I woke up several times that night, always when Gideon was squeezing my body closer to his, and it heated me up every time. I squeezed him in return and let my hand roam his back, his arm, and down to his ass. It became our little routine; he responded in kind and touched me too. He kissed my chest and my neck, and he dared to grope my ass for about five seconds before he shifted to safer ground.

It was a bit maddening, but mostly, I just loved the warmth and sharing a bed with another man again.

"You feel good," he whispered sleepily.

"So do you." I stifled a yawn and pressed my lower body to his. It was a shame he'd left his boxer briefs on.

He was half hard just like I was, and hey, I was still a red-blooded male. He turned me on. I didn't have to fake shit.

At some point during the night, he'd moved higher up so we were face-to-face, and I was tempted to ask him if I could remove the mask. But in the end, I didn't have to, because he removed it for me. I blinked drowsily, both dreading and hoping I'd see him.

I didn't see squat. Not even the freaking silhouette of him or the contours of his face.

It was probably for the best. Right now, he was a living, breathing fantasy. His body felt amazing next to mine, and I was seriously hooked on his voice.

"You wanna sleep some more?" I combed my fingers through his hair and scratched his scalp lightly. Judging by the hum of pleasure that emanated from his chest, he liked it.

"I think so. Lying next to you is highly distracting, but I don't want to overwhelm myself."

"Sleep, it is. There's no rush."

He relaxed at that and hitched my leg over his hip.

I wondered if he was planning on spending the whole night here every time or if he'd sometimes leave once he'd done whatever he came for. I guess I'd thought he'd at least wanna get off tonight. We weren't seeing each other again until Tuesday night. On the other hand, if he'd gone his entire adult life so far without exploring with men, two days was nothing.

CHAPTER 3

"You seem distracted," Tina mentioned over the phone.

"Sorry. I've been tryna beat this level for a week," I muttered, making my next move on the board. Whenever I had spare time, I had a minor addiction to games on my phone.

Tina huffed. "You have me on speaker so you can play stupid games while you're talking to me? I think I'm offended."

I grinned and scratched my nose, then moved one tomato toward two others. "Anyway. You sure you don't wanna share some innocent information about my client?"

Gideon was due in a little under an hour, and he'd sent me new instructions. The rule on silence was back; he didn't want me to speak unless it was absolutely necessary. Sleep mask on, but he'd remove it once we were hidden away in darkness. And I'd been told to be naked and on all fours on the bed upon his arrival.

His quick disappearance after our first night had disgruntled me. No goodbye or anything. He'd snuck out while I'd been asleep, and not a word since then.

I didn't know why I'd expected any messages, to be honest. He hadn't done anything wrong.

Either way, I was curious about this man. But to no one's surprise, Tina didn't wanna share shit.

Oh, other than our test results being back. We were good to go.

"I think I'm curious about him because he draws out my protective side," I mused. "I wanna help him, you know?"

"Honey, you've been intrigued by the anonymous ones for as long as I've known you," Tina responded.

True to an extent, but there was something more to it when I was with someone who struggled in one way or another. Society's outcasts, those who couldn't be themselves without a million layers of bullshit and pretending—I'd always had a soft spot for them.

"I'm having drinks with one of my new girls now, Nicky. Can we chat more tomorrow?"

"Yeah, sure, of course." I could hear her paying the cab fare in the background, so I waited until she was done before I wrapped up the call.

A glance at the alarm clock on the nightstand told me I had twenty minutes before Gideon got here.

Might as well keep playing my game. I had plenty of other things to do but nothing I'd finish in that short amount of time. Tomorrow I had four students who'd requested a rock song to learn on their instruments, and I was kinda tempted to pick one of mine or Anthony's. He'd sent me a new one to go through today, a rough recording, and we'd probably rehearse it this Friday when we had access to our local church.

My brother was a lot more involved than I'd ever be, but I

freaking loved collaborating with the choir. And there were no better acoustics than in a church.

I should put up a note about the rehearsal on Friday so I didn't make other plans. Ruby and I were meeting up for happy hour tomorrow, and she often had suggestions. Leaving my phone on the bed, I walked over to the kitchen and grabbed my notebook, flipping past the pages that were riddled with lyrics, thoughts, and doodling, until I found a blank page.

I jotted down the time, the church, the day, and the reminder to ask Anthony to bring my amplifier.

Hopefully there would be time to have a talk with him too, 'cause though I hadn't listened to his new song yet, the title, "Bottom of a Heartbreak," made me wanna put my foot down.

He was gonna insist that the lyrics weren't personal, and I was gonna call bullshit.

After attaching the note to the fridge, I made my way back to the alcove and threw myself on the bed. Everything was ready for Gideon's arrival. Duvet rolled down, all lights off except for the one on the nightstand, curtains closed, and I was as naked as the day I was born.

At two minutes to ten, I gave up on trying to beat that fucking level. I was gonna see pears and tomatoes and honey-combs in my dreams at this point. One of the students had gotten me hooked on the game, but it just made me pissy.

All right. Blindfold on. Nothing else to do but put my ass in the air for Gideon.

Tonight wasn't my night. I felt unsettled and antsy. This was work. I'd been mad comfortable this past Saturday, and I'd even wondered if Gideon and I could have some amazing chem-istry. It hadn't felt farfetched at all. Almost like it was right there, crackling, smoldering, waiting for us to act on something that went beyond cuddling. But now I was having doubts. Half my brain was still at the academy in Brooklyn—and with my brother.

I needed to get out of my head—

A key turned in the lock.

I took a deep breath and tried to shake the rest of the day off me.

Gideon let himself in and locked the door. Same sounds as last time. A kitchen chair was pulled out, and I assumed he hung his coat or suit jacket there.

He didn't sit down on the edge of the bed first this time, though. I heard him unbuckle his belt and pull down his zipper, and it was as hot as it had been on Saturday.

"You're my toy, and you don't talk back."

Welp. *Hot. As. Fuck.*

"Unless something is wrong," he added hastily.

I grinned to myself.

Was it weird that I found his uncertainty adorable and charming? It drew me in and stole my entire focus.

He crawled onto the foot of the bed and came up behind me, and it killed my humor. I was itching to find out what he had in store for me. More than that, I wanted to get him off and see how he'd react. But I knew the seeing part wouldn't happen, because one of the last things he'd said to me during our first night was that he felt more comfortable without an audience, including me. He'd guessed, or rather stated, that I knew he wasn't experienced, to which I'd nodded, and that seemed to bother him.

Even as a beginner, he wanted to come off as assertive. Life didn't work that way.

He touched me with more ease today, thankfully. His hands roamed my back and sides, slowly inching down to my ass.

Had he dropped all his clothes yet?

"I want to use you," he murmured.

I'm yours to use, honey.

"Almost like a doll..." He drew a single finger between my ass cheeks, and I flushed all fucking over. Where was this confidence coming from? "My God," he whispered. "I've been thinking about this since I left."

I swallowed.

The way he slowly, cautiously circled my ass drove me nuts. There was something indecent about his innocent exploration of me.

Next thing I knew, he lowered his head to kiss me there, and my eyes flashed open behind the sleep mask. He'd completely thrown me off guard. Weren't we missing a whole bunch of steps? First base, second base... Fuck if I knew, but I didn't think it was supposed to go from cuddling to tongue-fucking someone's asshole.

Tongue-fucking was extreme, but he wasn't shy, that was for sure. He dropped openmouthed kisses and pushed the tip of his tongue inside me, all while his long fingers kneaded my cheeks.

I had to swallow a moan when he reached under me and cupped my balls.

The blood in my body surged downward, and I had to lock my elbows into position.

"I masturbated in the car ride on the way over," he admitted.

Jesus fucking Christ.

Was he a deviant in sheep's clothing?

"I kept thinking of you riding me," he went on, trailing his kisses higher up now. "It's one of my biggest fantasies, you riding my cock in the back seat."

That could be arranged in the right type of car.

I shivered incessantly as he kissed his way up my spine and wrapped his fingers around my cock.

"It feels so good to say these things out loud." He planted his forehead against my back and breathed shallowly. "I wish I could touch you in public without people knowing what's going on."

An inexperienced man with bottled-up exhibitionist fantasies. This could get wild.

"Sometimes I just want my hands down your pants," he said quietly. I bit back a groan. He stroked me unhurriedly from base to tip, twisting his grip slightly, then down again. "I want to see you come. Lie down on your back."

I didn't hesitate for a second. I turned around and dropped onto my back, and Gideon crawled over me so he was straddling my thighs.

"I made you this hard," he whispered, seemingly to himself. "I can say whatever I want, and you won't answer. You don't realize how liberating that is. To not have to think twice about every word that comes out of my mouth." He stroked me a little faster and tightened his grip, and I had to grit my teeth to hold back any noises. "My sexy, beautiful little toy. I'm going to fuck every hole possible in your body."

He was killing me.

His breathing was coming out faster, making me wonder if he was stroking himself at the same time. It felt like that should be my job.

"You don't understand," he muttered. "The past two days, I've felt the levees break within me, figuratively speaking. When I say every hole possible, I mean it. Like sliding my cock between your buttocks until I come all over them. Like slowly pushing inside your wet mouth. Like sleeping with my cock buried in your ass."

Fuck me!

I sucked in a breath, then smashed my lips together. I went rigid. If I didn't tense up, I'd move. I'd fucking throw myself at him. I'd moan, plead, and gasp.

"I think I want the first one I mentioned right now," he said, out of breath. "Turn around again, please. I have this vision stuck in my head, and I can't get it out." He kept talking while I scrambled into position on my stomach. "I want to see the come spurt out of my cock and soak you."

I did the only thing I could do—I buried my face in the pillow and screamed internally.

Holy hell, where had this man come from?

"You can't come yet," he warned, pushing his cock between my ass cheeks. Then he pressed them together, creating a tight sleeve for his slick cock. Whether it was lube or pre-come, I didn't know, but it was maddeningly hot. "This is what I've fantasized about for so long. A lovely boy existing for my needs." He let out the sexiest groan I'd ever heard, and I could almost cry. I was so goddamn hard. "I'm going to take care of you too."

Please do, before I come on the sheets like a preteen.

He started panting. "I want to sleep between your legs with your cock in my mouth. That's my plan, and I won't let you distract me."

I tried so hard, but I couldn't stop a whimper from slipping out between my lips, the low sound hopefully muffled by the pillow. He was seriously killing me. My cock hurt, my balls ached, a sharp current of sheer horniness buzzed through me without an end in sight, and my lungs burned for air.

Then he stopped. Or slowed down. And with a rough, raspy moan, he jerked forward and started coming. Hot splashes of his come landed along my spine.

I wanted to scream.

My mind was swimming in images of what I was desperate for, and I lost my mental footing. I existed in a place of decadent fantasies, and I reached for them all. Him fucking me hard, me deep-throating him, him nursing from my cock, me on my knees, our bodies intertwined, sweaty fucking, pleading moans, and twisted sheets.

Gideon called me a filthy mess as he slipped his cock out from between my ass cheeks, and then he told me he was going to clean me up.

"Lie still. I'll be back."

I counted the seconds.

I tried to unclench, but I couldn't. I hadn't even noticed I was white-knuckling the sheet.

When he came back, he dragged a warm washcloth over my lower body, and it took all my willpower not to squirm and push into his touch. Thankfully, he didn't leave. Once he was done, he threw the washcloth somewhere, then rolled me over, and in a fluid motion, he joined me in bed and sucked my cock into his mouth.

The relief and the pleasure exploded inside of me, and I moaned. I moaned loudly. I broke the rules and threaded my fingers into his hair; I eased my cock deeper into him, and I acted like a desperate slut. To be fair, I fucking was.

"I'm sorry, can't help it," I gasped. "Fuck, that's amazing."

I could tell he'd probably never done this before, but it just worked. It felt so damn good, and he sucked me hard and wetly. No one needed finesse and grace. Or rhythm, for that matter. All that existed was my cock in his mouth—and his tongue. Madonn', how he used his tongue.

"Close," I groaned.

The ball of desire dropped lower and lower, and a tingling sensation rushed down my spine.

He didn't stop sucking me.

I couldn't warn him again. My orgasm crashed down on me, and my whole body protested as I tensed up more than I already had. I screwed my eyes shut behind the mask, I held my breath, and I started coming. Bursts of come coated the roof of his mouth. He prolonged my climax by gripping the base of my cock tightly, almost too tightly, but the way he sucked the release from me and made the sexiest, greedy humming sounds intensified the bliss.

As the orgasm subsided, all strength left my body. My hands fell to my sides, and I couldn't move a muscle.

Oh my God.

I sucked in a sharp breath and waited for my heart to stop pounding.

Still couldn't move. I'd officially melted into the mattress.

I swallowed dryly. "Do I have to be quiet?"

He nodded with my softening cock in his mouth. Then he repositioned me on my side, and he stayed next to me, seemingly comfortable down there. His tongue swirled around me sluggishly, sensually, and it drew another shudder from me.

Was he serious? He was gonna sleep now? Like that?

It was hot and felt freaking fantastic, obviously, but I kind of wanted cuddles. And kissing. I wanted to kiss him. Hell, I wanted to worship his feet, and that wasn't my kink.

He hummed and pressed the head of my cock between his tongue and the roof of his mouth.

I sighed in contentment, exhaustion creeping in, and wove my fingers through his hair again. I loved the feel of it.

"It's a little cold," I admitted.

Gideon released my cock and responded by pulling up the duvet and covering most of my body with it. Then he snuck under it himself and gathered my leg over his middle.

"Give me a pillow, please," he said.

I reached blindly for one and pushed it down the mattress.

He'd been serious. He'd made himself a little spot there, and he was gonna sleep while nursing from me.

"Your cock is perfect," he murmured between soft kisses. "It belongs in my mouth."

Yeah, okay. I scrubbed a hand over my jaw and yawned.

These two months were suddenly looking a lot more interesting, even to me, 'cause fuck if I'd done this before.

Gideon was something else.

I stayed in Brooklyn after working late on Friday and coerced my brother into having dinner with me at our favorite diner. It was this shitty little dive in Prospect Park where the two owners had never been able to agree on the interior design. So it was part fifties diner with checkered floors, red faux-leather boots, and a jukebox, and part rock 'n' roll hangout with old guitars and posters on the walls. They had cheap beer, the best wings in New York, and decent cheesecake.

We ordered two baskets of wings, beer, and fries before Anthony told me to spit it out.

"Huh?" I cocked my head.

He offered a come-on look. "You've been restless all day. Somethin's buggin' ya."

He wasn't wrong.

"You better not regret covering more classes," he said.

"I'm not." I showed my palms. Hell, quitting at Starbucks and Applebee's had been the best thing happening this year. It freed up most of my time and allowed me to work at the academy almost full time. "I gotta talk to someone about my client, and you're my favorite." I batted my lashes.

He snorted and hauled out a few notebooks from his messenger bag. The leather was worn and weathered from years of use. It'd been a birthday present from Pop once.

Anthony flicked me a glance. "He treats you all right, doesn't he?"

"Yeah, no, it's not that." I didn't know where to start, and the server was on his way with our beer, so I waited.

Tuesday, Wednesday, and Thursday had shown me a side of Gideon that was both sexy as sin and frustrating. Yesterday, he'd fucked me for the first time, and the same rules had applied. No talking, barely any moving, and I wasn't allowed to see him.

He got me off just fine and was equally demanding and giving; he was both rough and gentle. In that respect, he was sort of a fantasy come true. But the rules, man...fucking hell, I hated them.

I nodded in thanks and took a swig of my beer before the foam had disappeared.

Then I wiped my mouth and took a breath. "He won't let me do anything," I said. "If it'd been his kink to mess around with a fuck doll, I'd understand better, but to explore...? I don't know. It feels like there's another reason why he doesn't want me to move or say anything."

"Rewind—wait. You're not allowed to talk or move?" Anthony's forehead creased with confusion.

I shrugged. "I wear a sleep mask too. I don't know what he looks like." The whole situation was difficult to explain. "Here's the thing. He's..." I scratched my forehead quickly, racking my brain for the right words. "He both takes and gives a lot. He's seriously addictive with how he uses me, but it's like he's not interested in participation. Which is kinda fucking important when you explore something new, if you ask me. I mean, isn't that the point? Figuring things out *with* someone?"

"Hm." His short hum was so him. It was usually followed by a long spiel about things I had to consider.

It made me scramble. "He's kept his sexuality hidden for what I assume is most of his life. Our first night together ended with a seven-hour-long cuddling session, and he told me he was tired. Like, mentally wrung out. I think he's...you know, insecure and uncertain. It comes out here and there. And if I talked or were a more active participant, maybe it would change the path he's on."

He tilted his head at that last bit. "He could be trying to prevent chaos. You know James at the academy—we gotta email him clear-cut instructions, notes, and the songs he's going to work on beforehand so he can mentally prepare himself. The smallest change in his schedule throws him off."

Legit. James was a talented pianist and found peace in music. He'd been with Anthony since he was a little kid. Now he was a senior in high school who would probably get accepted into Juilliard. But as Anthony had mentioned—the smallest change could ruin the kid's day and catapult him into panic.

Was that why Gideon was so strict with the rules?

"Maybe he's trying to save face," I realized out loud.

"Who?"

"My client. Yeah, because—yeah, he indicated that he doesn't wanna come off as a beginner who doesn't know what he's doing."

Anthony quirked a wry smirk. "He wants to achieve the impossible. Good luck with that."

"Exactly," I replied. "And it's robbing him of a more genuine experience. By keeping me out of the interaction, he won't feel like he's actually explored anything."

He tipped his hand, weighing his response, and shrugged a little. "That's his choice, bambino. I know you wanna get involved in everything, but sometimes it just isn't your place."

I stared at him, wholly unsatisfied with his remark. The fuck? I didn't wanna get involved in *everything*.

He pointed at me. "You wanna fix other people's problems, and don't even try to deny it."

I opened my mouth to argue, only to snap it shut and narrow my eyes at him. Motherfucker! I was suddenly on trial for wanting to help people? Get outta here with that shit.

Anthony chuckled.

I shook my head, disgruntled, and glanced out the window. It'd been dark when we'd left work, and now the Friday night crowd was coming out to have dinner. As I checked the time on my phone, I saw we had two hours to kill before we had rehearsal at our church in Williamsburg.

Maybe Nonna would stop by. She liked to watch us play.

Our food arrived, and my stomach snarled with approval. I doused my wings in buffalo sauce.

"Speaking of solving other people's problems," I said, "let's talk about your new song, which is clearly about you tryna find excuses to stay with someone who doesn't make you happy."

He frowned at me. "How the fuck did you draw that conclusion?"

I rolled my eyes. "Let's see. You're at the bottom of a heartbreak, you gotta learn to love what you have, you ask for time and space, there's nowhere to go, you feel trapped—do I need to go on?"

"For chrissakes, it's just a song, Nicky." He shot me an irritated look before digging into his food.

It was clear he didn't wanna talk about it, so I made a compromise with myself. If Nonna showed up at the church later and heard the song, I wouldn't have to say another word on the matter because she would. She hated how Shawn used Anthony. Besides, where was he tonight? It was Friday, and Anthony's exciting plans involved dinner and band practice with his kid brother. I was willing to bet Shawn had plans in the city with his clubbing buddies. Like he did most weekends.

If he ever showed up for Sunday dinners, he did it hungover.

My phone buzzed on the table, and I checked it after wiping my hands on a napkin.

Huh. A message from Gideon. I'd given him my number but never thought he'd use it.

Hello. This is Gideon. I was wondering if we could meet up more often. Every time I show up at the studio, I try to remind myself that we have time. I repeat to myself, "We have till dawn," "We have two months," but I'm still experiencing some anxiety about how quickly time passes. You would be compensated generously.

I couldn't show Anthony the screen fast enough. I wanted to yell, "Can't you see?!" But instead, I said, "Don't tell me this man doesn't want something genuine. He's just uncertain about how to achieve it—and he thinks he can be satisfied with an arrangement where he pulls all the strings. He thinks having me as some puppet is enough."

Anthony scanned the message. "We have till dawn." He smiled faintly. "That's sweet." Then he lifted a shoulder and finished another wing. "Maybe he does want more. I never said he didn't. My argument is that it's not your place to give it to him. No pun intended."

Something in me deflated, and it was because of my brother. This wasn't him. He thought I had a bleeding heart? Forget about it. The whole reason he'd started his academy was to help and inspire children through music, and he had a soft spot for those who found peace in whatever music had to offer.

He'd gone above and beyond to help out his entire life. He'd picked up the pieces of Pop after our mother died of cancer. I'd been too young to remember, but Anthony had tackled Pop, his own grief, and school at the same time. He'd fought for the underdog, the bullied kids, the outcasts. For crying out loud, he was a Mets fan.

Fuck both him and Gideon. I was gonna help them whether they wanted me to or not.

Sorry sacks of shit.

I lowered my gaze to my phone and typed out a response.

I can be available on Mondays and/or Sundays too, but if you choose Sunday, I'd prefer to meet up at eleven instead of ten.

Sunday dinner at Nonna's was usually over around eight, but she was incapable of saying goodbye, so we tended to stand in the hallway for half an eternity while she came up with just one more thing to say or do before we left. It always involved handing over leftovers and telling us who in the neighborhood was pregnant or getting divorced.

Gideon replied quickly.

What about tonight? I'd like to see you tonight.

The man didn't wanna come off as inexperienced, but he had no issues showing vulnerability or being honest with how eager he was.

I can't tonight. My brother and I are rehearsing some songs with the choir at our local church in Brooklyn.

I threw a couple fries into my mouth as Gideon wrote his response.

My eyebrows flew up when I read it.

I saw the note on your fridge and let it slide because it's your home for the moment. Same with the drumsticks I saw by the door and your keyboard by the window. But try not to share any information about yourself. I want this arrangement to be as impersonal as possible. I'll take both Mondays and Sundays, thank you. 11 p.m. for

Sunday sounds good. I will handle the compensation through Tina.

Oh, fuck you, dude.

Sorry if my personal life got in the way of your—

My thoughts were derailed when another of his texts popped up.

And please don't leave any more notes on the table. If I sneak out while you're asleep, it's for a reason. You don't have to tell me goodbye or anything. I will see you tomorrow, then.

Now he was pissing me off. I'd left a single note with my phone number on it, and I'd written, "In case you're gone before I wake up, my number if you need it." Since I didn't bring the iPad out with me.

Maybe I shouldn't get involved. He seemed to have made up his mind about everything.

CHAPTER 4

I t felt good to be back in the church I'd spent so many boring hours in growing up. It wasn't every day we got to practice with the choir; I think last time was before summer. Now, Halloween and Thanksgiving were right around the corner, and the choir had some fun events to rehearse for. Anthony and I would be part of one of them.

Back in the day, it'd been mostly older people in the choir—and by older, I meant Anthony's age—but now several of them were even younger than me.

It was a representative mix consisting of twenty men and women of the Catholic population of Williamsburg, and I'd gone to school with many of them. Anthony could say the same for the older folk.

As much as I loved Manhattan, this was where I belonged. It was home. With all its flaws.

"Nicky, can you take the piano for warm-up?" Anthony

asked. "We have Nina, Henri, and Luiz on bass, guitar, and drums. I'll take the organ."

"Sounds good." I left my guitar with him at the first pew and headed up toward the piano. "Maria!"

She was a friend of ours; she lived in the same building as Nonna, and I could always borrow the sheet music from her.

"What's this I hear about you leaving Brooklyn, papi?"

"It's just temporary." I smiled, sitting down at the piano. A handful of people had arrived and taken their seats along the pews. "What're youse working on these days?"

She smirked knowingly and handed over a binder. "It's all in here."

"Cheers, hon." I found a good one to begin with, X Ambassadors' gospel song "Belong," and the choir fell quiet as I played the first few notes.

Anthony took his seat at the organ across the aisle and nodded to me, so I started over and signaled to Nina, Henri, and Luiz.

One of Anthony's buddies, Matthew, stepped forward to the mic that was set up for whoever was doing a solo.

His voice had great range, and he handled the higher notes almost as well as my brother did.

As soon as the choir filled in and flooded the small church with their harmonies, it became abundantly clear that this was exactly what I needed tonight. And even more so when I gazed out over the pews and spotted my grandmother. I smiled at her, and she waved enthusiastically and sat down somewhere in the middle.

After two glasses of brandy, Nonna liked to brag about our music abilities and how they came from her. She'd once been a singer herself, and she'd bought Anthony his first guitar.

We ran through a handful of songs with the choir, most of

which would be performed at the church's fall concerts, and then we started going through the program for the event we were gonna participate in. It was an annual outdoor event that took place in an abandoned church that was more ruins than church. The lot sat on the edge of the neighborhood, and people tended to walk past it a little faster at night. But for one day of the year, the area was packed. The ruins of the church were lit up with bistro lights and spotlights and candles, people brought their own chairs and blankets, and a few members of the community sold hot beverages, cookies, hot dogs, and candied almonds.

As Anthony walked up to the choir and discussed harmonies of his new song, I sat back and listened on one ear while my gaze scanned the visitors. I exchanged another smile with Nonna, but she was busy chatting to some woman I didn't know but recognized. Probably a neighbor. Judging by Nonna's gesturing and the way she patted the woman's arm, Nonna was giving unsolicited advice about something. She was fantastic at that.

Damn, Mr. Colinetti was here with his wife. He was my old math teacher in high school, and more importantly, Anthony's first crush.

That was another thing that didn't make sense about Anthony's relationship with Shawn. My brother usually preferred older men. He'd spent his twenties chasing silver foxes, and now that he was one himself, he acted as if the roles suddenly had to be reversed. Shawn was young. Twenty-four or something.

Come to think of it, Anthony had brought Shawn home for Sunday dinner about a year ago, after my brother had bitched about getting old. He'd even dyed his hair for a few months before giving that shit up.

Maybe I should plant sexy silver foxes in Anthony's path.

He needed someone sweet who was as nurturing as he was, someone who didn't use him as a place to crash or source of income when "money's short." Because Anthony would never stop helping those who asked. Hell, I'd stayed in his guest room for almost two years, and not only did he not expect any rent, he said I could stay for as long as I needed. Obviously, I paid my way and pulled my weight around the house, but Shawn sure as hell didn't.

Cazzo, the dude bothered me. For some reason, I'd always felt protective of Anthony, even when it should be the other way around. I guess it was because, unlike him, I wouldn't be taken for a ride.

Yet, he said I had issues with a bleeding heart?

Fuck that nonsense.

I shook my head to myself and glanced—huh. I didn't recognize the man in the back of the church, and he didn't belong here. That was one fancy-ass suit. He didn't sit down like the other dozen folks either; he stood near the exit and just looked out of place.

"Nicky!"

"What?" I whipped my head toward Anthony and realized I'd zoned out. "Sorry."

He smirked faintly. "You ready to switch places?"

"Yes, boss." I rose from the piano and met him halfway where he handed me the sheet music for the guitar, though he knew I'd improvise a bit. Music was like cooking. If you followed the recipe religiously, you weren't using your heart.

We took a couple minutes to get ready; I plugged in my electric guitar and made sure I didn't have to tune it again, and Anthony warmed up his fingers on the keys of the piano. In the meantime, the choir practiced their cues, and Maria and three other women positioned themselves closer to the microphone.

It was a hauntingly beautiful song, but it wasn't the most

challenging one. Focus would be on Anthony's singing and the choir.

"We'll run through it without stopping a few times," Anthony instructed. "If you miss a cue, just jump in again."

There was a murmur of acknowledgment, and I exchanged a nod with him before I took the first few notes and eased us into the song.

It was up to Nonna now. She'd hear Anthony sing about feeling trapped, about trying to find a way to settle for second best, about...well, giving up, essentially.

I let my fingers slide over the strings and glanced across the aisle. Anthony had his head bowed when he played—when he sang from his heart. It was a sign. I knew this wasn't "just some song." Nonna would see it too.

His voice never failed to capture my attention, and with the choir in the background, it was shivers all around. He sang of having nothing to say, having nowhere to go, and I wanted to say there was; he just needed to get up and dust himself off and try again.

The music quieted down until it was just my guitar, and that was when Anthony raised the tempo and sang louder. It was his thing. Ending one verse with peace, beginning the next with force.

The harmonies from the choir gave me goose bumps, and I looked out over the pews to see the response from the people watching. And my gaze landed on the strange man in the suit who remained standing in the doorway.

Feeling trapped...

Nothing to say...

Nowhere to go...

Anthony wasn't the only one hiding, the only one settling.

I was an idiot. There was no way it was him.

Right?

Gideon had told me he was six-four or something, hadn't he? He had a lot of money and could afford all things bespoke. Dark hair, brown eyes. I'd become intimately familiar with his body type. I'd heard the sound his dress shoes made on the hardwood floor in the apartment. But he wasn't standing in the doorway of a small church in Brooklyn right now. Not after the spiel he'd given me on not sharing personal information with him.

I lowered my gaze and closed my eyes, willing myself to concentrate on the song and nothing else.

We had five or six weeks left before the concert.

My fingers itched to put words to paper.

There was a reason I was so invested in Anthony's life, even in Gideon's life, and I was afraid it was to distract myself from my own sorry love life. Or lack thereof.

I couldn't worry about that right now, though.

As the song drew to a close for the second time, I opened my eyes again.

The man in the doorway had left.

Get back up, get back up again.

I hummed to myself as I prepared my, oh...third ice cream sundae for the day. I went with strawberry this time, along with enough chocolate sauce to cover the ice cream, then a dozen maraschino cherries and a couple chocolate-filled wafers.

Then I went back to my keyboard and sat down. I had another half hour or so to develop the song I was working on before I had to get ready for Gideon's arrival. I'd been at it all day, unable to get Anthony's song out of my head. It deserved a response.

You'll find strength in the fight.

"Hmm." I stuck the ice-cream-filled spoon into my mouth and jotted down the words in my notebook.

I wanted to believe that the best kind of love was worth burning for. A flicker of a flame wasn't enough. It had to consume you. I wanted the blood, sweat, and tears kind of love. The unpredictable, the wild, and the hard love.

Hard love.

We were always proud of hard work. We stood taller next to our biggest achievements.

Hold on tight.

The music swept through me, and I played until the perfect melody emerged. I'd continue working on it tomorrow, though I suspected my mind would be preoccupied with it all night. Hey, Gideon wanted me passive and motionless; he was gonna get it. I'd just wander off mentally instead.

Or, I was gonna get through to him somehow. I kept going back and forth. He'd texted me the instructions for tonight, and he wanted me lying naked on my side when he arrived. Sleep mask on until the lights were off, and then he'd remove it. He'd thought of me all day, he'd said, and he wanted to be inside me within a minute of his getting here, so I had to prepare myself too.

He was taking the excitement out of this arrangement mad fast.

I was officially nothing more than a sex doll, and it made it difficult to motivate myself to help him.

That rock made a comeback in the pit of my stomach tonight, and now I knew it had nothing to do with my job as a sex worker. It wasn't about sex, it wasn't about selling it, it wasn't about feeling "dirty." It was because of clients like Gideon.

Every now and then, someone had rented my services to treat me like an object, and that did it. That was the reason.

Gideon hadn't been lying. He'd been inside me within a minute of his arrival, and he'd been different. He hadn't spoken a word until he'd gotten off about two minutes ago. And then, he'd only said, "I'll be right back."

He'd disappeared, only to return with a wet washcloth to clean me off.

I was so done with this. Now I remembered why I'd quit in the first place.

Seven weeks to go.

Seven weeks of evidently not feeling like a human being whenever my client popped in for a quiet fuck.

At least Tina had gotten me a sweet deal with the payment renegotiation. Now I'd be walking away with four grand a week, minus her ten percent. First payment was due tomorrow, which Tina had held for me. The client paid in advance; the sex worker got paid afterward.

"You didn't get hard during..." Gideon's voice filled the dark apartment, and it faded just as quickly.

I had nothing to say. He hadn't asked a direct question.

I scrubbed my hands over my face and yawned, hoping he'd either leave or wanna get some sleep, because I was a few minutes away from losing the last fuck about the rules. And if I opened my mouth now, he'd get an unfiltered piece of my mind.

The mattress dipped with his weight as he sat down on the edge next to me. "I'm frustrated. I know the rules I've imposed, but now I feel alone in this companionship."

"Because you are." Welp, those words left me of their own volition. But now I might as well continue. "You asked for a plaything who didn't move or speak and you got one."

I heard him swallow and take a couple breaths.

"Have...Have I hurt you?" he asked hesitantly.

Yes, I wanted to say, but it wouldn't be right. He hadn't done anything wrong whatsoever. I just wasn't as perfectly suited for this work as I'd once thought I was, and now I was out of the game. Two years had passed since this had been a regular thing. My guard was down. I'd been naïve to think I could jump in without any preparations.

"I've hurt myself a little," I settled for saying. "I thought I could go through with an arrangement—as a one-time thing—like I used to. This was once my full-time job, but I quit two years ago."

"Yes, Tina explained she was pulling someone out of retirement who matched my criteria."

That was one way of putting it.

Gideon cleared his throat. "Are you saying you can't go through with it? I'm not good at reading between the lines."

I blew out a breath and sat up. We were doing this. We were gonna talk. "No, I can." Because fuck all other options. I was not going back to fucking Applebee's. "What I can't do is play along with your stupid rules. It's not genuine, Gideon. You wanna explore for real? Let me see you. Let me participate. Don't put a freaking gag order on me."

I was met by silence, and it wasn't like I could see him. It was so frustrating.

"It wouldn't kill you to have a simple conversation with me," I went on. "We can do it on your terms—we can text each other for all I care if you don't wanna talk verbally. Whatever you're the most comfortable with, but this...?" I gestured between us, even though he couldn't see it. "This is about as real as you exploring with a blow-up doll."

The silence stretched on, but I could sense him processing what I'd said. It sounded like he scrubbed at his face, and he breathed easier. There was surrender in his sigh. He had to realize what we'd done so far wasn't working. Not for two months. It wasn't what he wanted, and it sure as hell wasn't what I wanted.

"It's...difficult...maneuvering, for lack of a better word, this arrangement," he said slowly, seemingly struggling to phrase himself. "Normal people can multitask and try on various hobbies different days of the week, but I go all in. I almost obsess over something until I've figured it out, and I can't do that with you. I've made promises. I have commitments. This is supposed to be purely physical, and...and that's why I don't want to see notes on the fridge about where you're going on Friday. I don't want to know that you play the keyboard and the guitar and God knows what else, because I get intrigued."

I pinched my lips together and cocked my head.

My guitar case had been under the bed the entire time I'd stayed in this apartment.

Fucking hell, I had to see him. I was done with this. I understood his worries; I genuinely did, and I'd heard similar stories from some of Anthony's students. About the obsessing, about multitasking. But he was paying me to give him a full experience of exploring his sexuality, and I was itching to break the number one rule. The client being in charge.

I could hear Anthony's warning about not getting involved as I reached for the lamp on the nightstand.

Please don't panic, please don't panic.

I shouldn't do this. Before I pressed the switch, I knew it was wrong. It should be his choice.

I still flipped it, and the apartment flooded with a dim light.

I knew it.

Gideon sucked in a breath and looked away, but he remained sitting there. He didn't leave. He balled his hands into fists, and his breathing sped up. No panic, though. Anxiety was part of life; doing something scary wasn't necessarily bad, so that wasn't going to stop me.

He was a stunning man of lean muscle, broad shoulders, and some silver at his temples. Nothing about him was small. My ass could testify... But it was time to see the rest of him.

"Sometimes you have to put yourself first," I murmured. Moving slowly, I got up on my knees and shifted behind him. I brushed my hands up his arms and over his shoulders, and he shuddered. "I won't push further without asking for permission, okay?" I didn't even sneak a glance at the window, where I knew I'd be able to see his reflection. "Can I touch you like this? And kiss you here?" I nuzzled his neck.

He smelled so fucking good.

"I suppose," he replied tightly. "This is highly unnerving."

"Unnerving is okay." I grazed my lips along his shoulder and peered down his front. Sexy chest, sexy chest hair, sexy thighs, sexy cock. "You're outside of your comfort zone. That shit's terrifying at times, but it ain't bad. It makes us stronger."

Funny how quickly the rock in my stomach crumbled into dust.

"I wanna ride that cock later."

He swallowed. "Oh. Okay."

I smiled against his skin and dropped an openmouthed kiss as I draped one arm over his shoulder to touch his chest.

"I, uh, I have fantasies about that," he said.

"I remember." Now I couldn't stop touching him. My hands roamed his torso greedily, and it felt so damn good to be unshackled. "You're a sexy man, Gideon. Out of this world sexy."

"Thank you. So are you."

I grinned. That sounded like one of those well-rehearsed, automatic responses he had in his arsenal. I'd heard a couple of them before.

"How are you feeling now?" I murmured.

He shivered. "Aroused and anxious."

I could work with that.

"Can I get on your lap?" I wondered. "You can close your eyes if you want."

He tensed up, and I was the jackass who focused on the definition of his muscles, but then he nodded jerkily, so hopefully his anxiety was manageable.

I made sure to touch him when I moved around him to get on his lap, just so he always knew exactly where I was. His eyes were closed, but I knew that handsome face. I'd seen it from afar last night.

Whereas I hadn't shaved in a few days and had some scruff going on, he was clean-shaven and rocked a sexy, cut jaw. There was something about sharp lines that drove me bonkers.

He drew a breath through his nose and clenched his jaw, and it looked like he was struggling to relax. In an attempt to help him, I guided his hands up my thighs. I wanted him to feel me the way I did him, now that we were finally in this together.

"I love seeing you." I cupped his jaw and leaned in, pressing a kiss to his cheek.

"You do?" He let out a shaky breath and tightened his grip on my hips.

"Fuck yeah. Who doesn't love seeing a gorgeous man?" I pressed my forehead to his and scooted a little closer, wanting his cock where it should be. "I think it's safe for you to open your eyes."

He shook his head minutely. "I don't want to see any judgment."

I furrowed my brow and inched back. "Why the fuck would I judge you?"

"I don't know. Society as a whole is judgmental. No one wants to be common, but everyone wants to be normal. We judge what sticks out and what we don't understand."

He wasn't wrong, and I couldn't imagine what it would be

like to try to fit into a bunch of boxes that weren't made for me on a daily basis. I'd gotten a taste of it when I came out to a few friends in school who hadn't already figured out I was gay, but that was about it. With my brother paving the way, I'd grown up in an accepting community, even with the church and old-school family members.

"I'm sure I've judged someone wrongly in my life," I admitted, smoothing my fingers over his brow. He appeared so troubled, and I didn't like it. "It's easy to think you get something just by imagining it. But you don't have anything to worry about with me, Gideon. I admire a person who will be true to himself and go after what he wants. That's what you're trying to do here, isn't it?"

He grimaced a little. "It's a compromise at best."

I hoped to hear more about it, because I was curious, but it would have to wait. Gideon was opening his eyes, and it felt like I'd been sucker-punched. He had the most soulful peepers I'd seen. Rich brown with gold and green flecks at the center, brimming with vulnerability and desire.

I smiled. "You were in Brooklyn last night."

He quickly broke eye contact and dropped his gaze to my shoulder, and fuck me if he didn't get a reddish tone to his cheeks. A grown man blushing—I'd seen everything now. And it was hella endearing.

"I told you I get intrigued," he replied defensively.

"Hey, I'm not complaining." I grinned and kissed the corner of his mouth. I wanted more; I wanted to kiss him properly. "Did you like what you saw?"

"No," he answered quietly. "It didn't satisfy my curiosity."

Nothing wrong with that in my book. I licked my lips, lingering close to his, and was done talking for the moment. Maybe he did too, because he took a trembling breath and closed the distance.

It sent a bolt of lust through me, and I locked my arms around his neck. We kept it tentative at first, letting the electricity flow between us with each soft brush, but when he applied some pressure, I let my body take the wheel and threw myself into the kiss.

Gideon was absurdly good at kissing. He didn't go too deep or too fast. I kissed him back hungrily, turned on by his sensuality, and quickly became hooked on the feel of his tongue along mine.

"Why do you taste of vanilla?" he asked, out of breath.

"I've had a shit-ton of ice cream today."

"Oh."

I smiled and snaked the tip of my tongue around his, at the same time as I wiggled my ass over his hardening cock. It was enough to derail his thoughts, and he reached for the lube on the nightstand.

I wouldn't need a lot of it. There was still some slickness from the last round.

This would be better, though. It already was.

"*Hngh.*" I bit down on my lip as he stroked two wet fingers over my ass. My skin was sensitive. "Fuck, that feels good."

He hummed and sank his teeth into my shoulder as he pushed both fingers inside, and I couldn't stop the moan. Experienced or not, he was ferocious and intense in the sack, and it was exactly the kind of sex I craved. It was real and instinctive.

Once I was ready, I lifted up while he gripped his cock, and then I slowly sat down on him. The burn felt different this time. It wasn't as sharp, and it wasn't tinged with cold detachment.

Gideon didn't groan expletives to express how good something felt. I noticed it in his touches and in his breathing pattern instead. He held me almost painfully tightly to him and buried his face against my neck.

"It's better when it's real, isn't it?" I combed my fingers through his hair and kissed his shoulder.

He nodded. "Amazing."

I tugged at his hair, pulling him back a bit, and captured his mouth with mine.

Now the actual exploring could begin.

CHAPTER 5

"I should get going," Gideon muttered drowsily.

"Mmm..." I stretched out next to him and threw a sleepy glance at the alarm clock. "It's only four. I thought we had till dawn."

He hummed and dipped down to kiss my chest. "Early meeting."

Late meetings, too, considering he'd arrived past midnight last night.

Three weeks of my arrangement with Gideon had turned me into a sex addict. Or a Gideon addict. He was still careful not to share anything about his personal life, so I hadn't shared anything either, though I could tell he had questions. Because now that we no longer disappeared in the darkness—mask gone, curtains open, lights on—I caught him scanning the apartment at times. He'd seen the sheet music I'd worked on at the table, the drafts I'd thrown on the floor, the constant presence of ice cream fixings on the kitchen counter, and the books on autism I'd borrowed from the library. But he never asked.

In turn, it'd made me wanna drop clues about myself, little teasers, which I knew would've been a dick move.

I wasn't actually gonna do it.

I wasn't gonna ask what he did for a living either, no matter how curious I was.

"Okay." I nudged him onto his back and kissed my way down his stomach. "Go to work, then."

I sucked his soft cock into my mouth and peered up at him.

My latest drug was his sleep-laden grin. It was fucking beautiful.

He'd relaxed around me so much lately, and I loved it.

"That's unfair." He sighed contentedly and closed his eyes. "I don't think I can come again."

Me either. We'd gotten three hours of sleep at the most. The rest of the time had been spent fucking, sucking, fingering, and making out like teenagers.

"I won't be late tonight," he murmured.

"Good." I swirled my tongue around his cock and pushed the head of him against the roof of my mouth.

He tensed up a bit and shook his head, then pushed himself up on his elbows. "Don't make me hard. You're too good at that."

I kissed the tip. "What if I don't obey like a good little boy?"

His gaze darkened, and he raked his teeth over his bottom lip. "You're a fantasy come true. And you want as much sex as I do."

I *had* noticed that he was freaking insatiable for his age. I'd read about it too. It wasn't uncommon for autistic people to be kinky or hypersexual, and Gideon certainly ticked both boxes. Speaking of, we should start living out a few of his fantasies. He had no issues talking about them.

The problem was, most of his fantasies took place in public. Gideon definitely had an exhibitionist in him.

"Do you wanna play with me in public tonight?" I asked, licking the length of his cock.

He groaned and fell back against his pillow again, and I couldn't help but grin victoriously. I loved having this effect on him.

"What do you suggest?" He scrubbed his hands over his face.

He was getting hard too.

"Wait," he said. "I know what we're going to do. Leave it to me." He pushed himself up once more and gestured for me to crawl over him. "Do you mind if people see you?"

I quirked a brow and straddled his stomach. "I'm not shy, if that's what you're asking." Truth be told, I wanted the surprise. "Don't tell me anything." I leaned down and kissed him softly. "If I have any problems with anything, I'll let you know."

"Good." He squeezed my ass tightly and kissed me back. "The filthier, the better."

I shivered as he grazed his middle finger over my opening. "Downright obscene, Daddy."

"Mmm, role-play..." He groaned and flipped me over. A somersault rocked my stomach as my back hit the mattress. "Maybe I need you one more time before I leave."

Maybe I needed him too. Another round, I meant. Not *him*.

When I took the elevator down to the street that night, I gave myself a pep talk after the minor nervous breakdown I'd had getting out of the shower earlier. Okay, it was possible I was being a drama queen, but this was something else. This was new. I'd spent three weeks in bed with Gideon, a mysterious rich dude with a perverted mind and some sort of confusion about his sexuality, and now I was leaving the apartment building to go somewhere with him.

I'd even paused to consider and reconsider what to wear, and that just wasn't me.

I wasn't uncultured; I'd had dates in restaurants with food that cost more than rent, and I wasn't a stranger to dressing up. But unless there was a dress code, I wore jeans and band tees.

I'd opted for a black Henley tonight. Anthony had given it to me because it'd been too tight for him.

I shouldn't be nervous. Based on the fantasies Gideon had talked about, we were either going for a dirty ride in his car, or we were going to a bar. Actually, there was a possibility we were going to an adult store too, though I wasn't sure he'd go for that yet. On the other hand, maybe that would be easier than a bar. At a bar, he'd have to pretend to converse with me, and that could get personal. God forbid.

I stepped out of the elevator and zipped up my jacket. At the end of the fifteen-or-so-feet-long hallway, I saw him. On the other side of the door, rather. He was leaning back against the car door, a car that didn't belong to him. He'd texted me earlier to let me know he'd be using Tina's chauffeur service, meaning we'd have a driver who got paid to keep his mouth shut, regardless of what he saw in the back seat.

I'd gotten the impression that Gideon wasn't unfamiliar with personal drivers, but I understood why he wouldn't use one of his own tonight. I wasn't sure, though. It was just another one of my theories about his private life. But yeah, I bet he had a driver. He was that kind of man.

Here we go.

Gideon glanced up from the sidewalk as I exited the building, and he flashed me a smirk tinged with nerves.

It settled some of mine.

"Imagine doing this with a sleep mask," I said.

His eyes flashed with humor. Then he opened the door for me. "Take a ride with me."

Yes, sir.

I climbed into the black SUV and immediately recognized the driver. We exchanged a subtle nod. He'd been working for Tina back in the day, too.

The back seat was...spacious. There was enough room for me to kneel at Gideon's feet if he wanted me to.

I hoped he wanted me to. The more sex, the better. It would save me from accidentally filling the silence with *chitchat*.

As soon as Gideon joined me and closed the door, the driver pulled away from the curb. The light in the car faded, and I was struck by a sense of awkwardness that I didn't like. I wasn't used to it. I wouldn't say I was the most confident guy out there, but I didn't take myself too seriously, and I was pretty easygoing.

Fuck, it was *my* job to make Gideon comfortable here.

I cleared my throat. "How was your day?"

That was innocent enough, and he could get away with a simple "Good."

"Long. Way too long." He drummed his fingers restlessly against his knee and peered out the window, making it abundantly clear that he felt the awkwardness too. "Lunch was inedible, and dinner wasn't much better."

I bit my tongue, literally. I wanted to ask him shit. I wanted to offer a shoulder if he needed one.

"Are you hungry?" I wondered.

He shook his head quickly and faced me. "Before you ask a second question, it's customary for me to ask how your day was. So. How was your day?"

I smiled, because I couldn't not. I thought he carried himself well and fit into our "normal" society most of the time, but whenever his peculiarities made themselves known, my sappy heart melted a little.

"It was good." I reached over the middle seat and grabbed his hand, threading our fingers together. "I did this and that, went here and there, and my lunch was awesome. So was my dinner."

I'd taken Nonna to Sahadi's for some shopping after a short day at work, and then I'd had dinner at her place while she had gossiped about people in the neighborhood.

Gideon stared at our hands and brushed his thumb over my knuckles. "You're comfortable with me."

That wasn't what I'd expected to hear. I cocked my head at him and wondered where his mind was at. Which...well, based on our brief history together, he was rarely mellow or in balance. I'd experienced him with anxiety and discomfort; I'd been with him when he was hard as a rock and thinking only of sex, and, recently, I'd seen him grin and chuckle, often when we were balls deep in cuddling and fighting off the cobwebs of sleep. But other than those precious moments, he alternated between horny and on edge, so it was close to impossible to guess his thoughts.

"I'm testing the waters," I corrected carefully. "I poke to see if now's a good time to push a limit or break a rule."

He frowned at me. "Why do you want to push my limits? That's not nice."

Heh. Yeah, well... No, he was right. It wasn't nice of me. "I'm curious about you," I admitted. "I like our chemistry and..." Fuck. What was I doing? Soon as I heard myself uttering those words, I knew I'd crossed a line. My own damn line. I was getting invested. "I'm sorry." I rubbed a hand over my mouth and glanced out the window. We were heading south along the west side. We'd just passed Chelsea Park. "I'll be on my best behavior from now on, I promise." I squeezed his hand but couldn't look his way yet.

It was rattling.

At the same time, there was an honest indifference within me that went, "So fucking what?"

So fucking what if I was genuinely interested in him? It happened.

"Change of plans," Gideon said abruptly. "Please take us to the corner of East 64th and Park."

My eyebrows flew up, and I turned toward him. What would we do on the Upper East Side? Considering our original direction, I had been leaning more toward the adult store option. The Village was full of 'em. But up by Central Park...? The only thing that belonged there was Gideon himself. He could probably afford a condo there.

"To answer your second question, I am, in fact, hungry," he told me tightly. And quietly. He was uncomfortable and restless again. His knee bounced, and his grip on my hand bordered on painful.

I played along for now. "What are you in the mood for?"

"French fries," he stated frankly. "I haven't had any yet this week."

It was Tuesday.

It was best to roll with the punches, because if he was in the mood for fries and had to go halfway across Manhattan to get some, he had very specific needs.

"I have a minor obsession," he muttered, facing the window. I stifled my amusement as best as I could. "Now you share something insignificant about yourself."

A flurry of excitement flew through me, and it made me shake my head to myself. This wasn't good, any of it. It was a two-month thing, and we only had five weeks left. A little less than that, even. But fuck it, right?

"I have a minor obsession with ice cream sundaes," I offered.

I caught his mouth twisting with mirth in the reflection of his window.

"I've seen the bowls in your sink," he said. "Doesn't look like a minor obsession."

I chuckled.

The streets blurred together in streaks of red, yellow, and green for the next few minutes as we shared likes and dislikes about "insignificant" things. He was a fan of taking long walks in the park with his dog; I was a fan of any day I didn't have to take the subway. His favorite season was the fall, and so was mine. He hated white wine but loved red. And chocolate; he really, really loved chocolate, but he didn't let himself have it often.

I hated wine, loved beer, loved chocolate, loved cookies—okay, I had a big sweet tooth—and I spent way too much money on sweet slices of heaven at Milk Bar. Gideon had never heard of the place, and the words were right there on the tip of my tongue, to offer to take him there...

Should I?

Pump the brakes a little.

I could compromise. "I'll pick up a box that we can share in bed when we've burned off a lotta calories this weekend."

He nodded once. "I'd like that very much."

His response was so formal, but I was getting better at understanding his signals now. He was struggling with the boundaries, struggling against them to do what he really wanted, and I had to admit that was why I wanted to break the damn rules. I could see sometimes that he was forcing himself to hold back, and I hated it. I wanted more for him.

He was more than just a client.

"Would you like me to turn, sir, or is it okay here?" the driver asked.

I glanced out and noticed we were here. The light was red, and we had time to jump out.

"Here's fine," Gideon responded. "I'll text when we're ready to leave."

"Yes, sir."

We left the car, and Gideon shut the door before he gestured up the sidewalk. "It's the storefront that glows green."

There could be only one spot on the otherwise dead street, and I wrinkled my nose automatically. It looked to be a small spot and hardly what one might call cozy, not that I'd expected it. Sterile was more appropriate. We walked closer, and all I could see was pristine white, lime-green booths, lime-green paint swirls on the walls, and the brightest of spotlights.

"You will notice how clean it is," Gideon said with a smile. "There isn't a grain of salt left behind on a single table. The minute you vacate your spot, someone cleans it."

Okay, so while the colors didn't seem to be up Gideon's alley, the cleanliness sure as hell was.

Gideon reached the door before I did, and he held it open for me.

It was a small establishment, with maybe ten or so booths and a counter with half a dozen stools, and the menu had a lot in common with any other fast-food joint. Except for it being more expensive here. A regular cheeseburger went for $12.99. Free soda with any purchase over five bucks, though!

"What would you like?" Gideon asked. "I can highly recommend the sliders and any fries."

Any fries... There were four kinds to choose from. Regular, steakhouse, battered, and curly, and you could choose to have them loaded or plain.

"I'll try the loaded regular ones, I think," I decided. "I had a big dinner at my grandmother's place, so I'm not very hungry."

"Loaded regular—excellent choice. Soda with that?" He stepped forward to order, and I requested a medium Coke.

There was only one other couple in here.

It was gonna be interesting to see what Gideon's agenda was. I grabbed some napkins, ketchup, and two straws from the condiment counter, then picked a booth in the middle. Something had triggered this change of plan of his, and I was wondering if it'd been my talk of chemistry and being interested. One could at least hope we'd talk more.

I assumed we came from two different worlds, but that didn't mean we couldn't be friends at the end of this arrangement.

I chewed on the inside of my cheek as a small voice in the back of my hopelessly romantic mind went, "Or maybe more."

It was dumb.

Tina hadn't been joking about my sad Facebook statuses. I didn't hate being single to the point where I'd jump into a relationship for the sake of it—far from it—but I *was* lonely. I hadn't been in a relationship in over a year.

Gideon tugged at my desire to have someone to take care of. I couldn't describe it in any other way than...it had to be chemistry. Because it wasn't something I'd felt with clients in the past.

When he came over with a tray and his eyes were glued to the fries, I couldn't help but smile. He wasn't watching his step or anything. It was all about the fries.

"Prepare yourself to be amazed." He sat down across from me and opened the paper container with the loaded fries for me. "I don't believe you will need ketchup."

"You can't have fries without ketchup." No matter how much cheese and jalapenos someone had dumped on top.

"You certainly can," he insisted firmly.

He'd picked a serving each of regular fries and battered fries for himself, and he was fucking adorable as he inserted a single fry into his mouth and closed his eyes in pleasure. He chewed slowly, and the way his jaw moved was nothing short of pornographic.

"Perfect crunch, every time," he mumbled to himself.

I grinned.

This was what I wanted. Decadent sex in all its glory, but I needed sex to be personal these days. It was partly what kept that rock out of my stomach. I wanted to get to know Gideon better. I wanted to see him like this, eating fries, not worrying about others' reactions or whatever molds he tried to fit into.

This was real.

I pulled a couple fries out of the melted cheese and threw them into my mouth, and I had to hand it to the man, he knew good fries. It was as if McDonald's and Burger King had a love child. The greasy saltiness from one, and the flavor and crunch from the other.

"So, is this your number one spot in the city?" I asked, wanting to start a conversation.

He shook his head and stuck a straw into his soda. "But it's possibly in the top ten." He offered a look of disdain when I dipped a fry into my ketchup. "I'm just going to ignore that."

I chuckled.

"What's your number one spot in the city?" he asked.

So, we were still exchanging the insignificant trivia bits. I was fine with that.

"The tourist magnets," I replied. "I love Times Square. I'll go there sometimes just to watch people. It's the center of the universe."

"I believe the center of the universe is—never mind. You weren't being literal." He cleared his throat and picked another fry. He was suddenly avoiding eye contact too, and he shifted uncomfortably in his seat. "I wanted to bring you here for a reason. You've mentioned breaking the rules, and I need to confess that I've already broken them. My curiosity got the best of me after I saw your rehearsal in Brooklyn, so I looked you up."

The words left him in a rapid rush, and then it was just silence. Even in my mind.

I didn't know how to react, to be frank. Part of me was flattered and relieved, because it meant he was interested too, though I didn't know how far that extended. Part of me was... surprised? Definitely. Either way, I wasn't angry, and he looked like he was expecting anger.

"All right." I sucked some salt off the edge of my thumb and smiled a little. "What exactly did you find out?"

He furrowed his brow. "That everyone calls you Nicky, not Nick. I found you on social media. You seem to be able to play countless instruments, and you're very close with your older brother. Unfortunately, your Instagram is set to private, so I only saw the few photos you have on Facebook."

Unfortunately.

I stifled my amusement as much as I could.

"You work as an instructor at The Fender Initiative, which appears to be a music school," he went on. "Your friend Ruby posts a great number of photos with you in them, and you like happy hour and trying new restaurants."

I let out a laugh, and I couldn't argue with him. Ruby had early shoots this month, so we hadn't been able to get together for drinks more than once or twice. It left us with quick lunches when she could duck out for half an hour. The other day, I'd met up with her outside the studio, and we'd tried the Indian place across the street.

"She's one of my best friends, but work doesn't allow us to hang out for very long," I responded, still amused. "My hours at my brother's academy are between noon and early evening, and hers are early mornings and/or late nights, so we grab food on the go, basically. We'll see each other often but rarely for more than twenty minutes."

"Sounds stressful," Gideon noted.

I shrugged and chucked some fries into my mouth. "And yes, my brother runs the music school where I work."

"You teach students to play instruments," he stated.

"Correct." I nodded and reached for my soda. "We have an exchange program going with two local schools, so that covers the early hours—at least for my brother. I only have a couple of those classes. Most of them start once regular school is out for the day."

He hummed. "How many instruments do you play?"

Damn. I had to think. I scratched the side of my head and squinted. "Um...maybe twelve?" Gideon's eyes widened, and I felt the need to clarify. "I'm not qualified to teach all of them," I said. "But I can get by."

"I see. And you prefer guitar and piano...?" he guessed.

"Definitely. And the drums. And the harmonica. And—okay, the list goes on."

He exhaled a chuckle and wiped his mouth on a napkin. "Do you sing also?"

"Sure. Not as well as Anthony, but I'm fairly good."

Gideon leaned back in his seat, observing me, and I dug it hard. I wanted his interest. I wanted him to keep asking me questions, because then it could be my turn later.

"You look up to him very much, don't you?"

"Every kid has a hero," I said. "He was mine. My pop and I are close, but it was Anthony who guided me through my childhood." Especially after Ma died. "He's...he's just a good role model." I lifted a shoulder, then smirked when a memory hit me. "He's the most resourceful man I know. For instance, when his first electric guitar broke and he couldn't afford a new one,

71

he picked the whole thing apart just to see how it was constructed. Then he used the parts that were still good and created a new guitar. It's something he still does."

"Impressive." Gideon leaned forward again and took some fries. "What kind of music do you play?"

I'd give him this topic. Once we were done with music, I wanted my go. "Soft rock, mostly. It depends what we're rehearsing for. The one you showed up at is for an outdoor concert in a few weeks, and since it's the church, it's mainly Christian rock."

He tilted his head and chewed and swallowed before speaking. "There will be a concert? One for the public?"

I mean...obviously? Wait, did he wanna go?

"Yes." I could ask him to come, though it felt a bit rushed. We weren't there—yet. But as always, there was a compromise. "I'll leave a note on the fridge with the details in case you wanna spy on me." I winked to show I had no ill feelings about his sneaking around.

Gideon flushed a little and busied himself with his fries.

Goddamn adorable.

"Can I ask the questions now?" I asked.

He had reluctance written all over, but he'd seen this coming. "It's only fair. Go ahead."

Fucking finally.

CHAPTER 6

Music was a safe route to begin with, or continue with, and he needed some warmin' up.

"What kind of music do you like?"

His shoulders lost some of their tension, and he thought about his reply while he polished off the rest of his battered fries. "I like many genres. The song I heard you and your brother perform with the choir was lovely—except for the lyrics, of course—but at home, I listen to progressive metal and classical music."

I lifted my brows, unsure of where to begin. What about the lyrics? And progressive *metal*? Madonn'.

Classical music made more sense with my profiling of him.

"What's wrong with Anthony's lyrics?" I asked first.

Gideon waved a hand, dismissive, and took a swig of his soda. "It was personal. It made me feel uncomfortable." Because it was a song about trying to settle for second best? About feeling trapped? "I enjoy music by musicians who do more than find a good beat. I appreciate technical songs. They take me on a journey, and I have to focus on the patterns."

That explained his appreciation for progressive metal, I guessed. Not to mention classical music.

I enjoyed technically progressive songs too, especially playing them, because I loved a good challenge. But there was still a side of me that disliked turning something complicated just for the fuck of it. Some songs were supposed to be easy. It had to be natural.

"Ironically, my all-time favorite song is a simpler one," he said. "My parents used to dance to 'Stand by Me' in the kitchen when I was very young. It stayed with me as one of my most cherished memories."

I smiled at that. "That's sweet. My brother and I have performed it a few times. We made it a lot more technical, though." I smirked.

"Really." He was too cute. It was clear he was holding back some of his curiosity, but I saw it in his eyes.

It made me more confident that I'd made the right decision not to outright invite him to the gig. Because he wasn't ready. We were still dancing around the carefully broken rules. Except, to him, it wasn't careful anymore. I wasn't spreading my legs for him in the studio apartment right now. I was here, on the Upper East Side, having fries with him.

I'd lubed him up for more personal topics now, I decided, and I knew just how to get there.

"I can admit that I didn't think you'd be the type of person who liked metal," I said.

People were always interested in knowing how others perceived them.

Gideon asked the obvious question. "What did you think I listened to?"

Almost there.

I chuckled softly. "I have a whole profile on you based on speculation. Tina didn't offer much, just that you wanted to explore something before you get hitched."

He flinched slightly at the last part but pressed forward and fell straight into my trap. "I'd like to hear about your profiling."

There we go.

Once I'd shared my perception of him, the sensitive subjects would be right there, hovering above us, and he could choose what to dissect.

"Let's see..." I sat back and pretended to ponder, as if I didn't already know exactly what to say. I'd only had weeks to think about this. "When Tina told me of your, uh, deal with your fiancée—then the fact that you're paying a crapload for everything—I automatically assumed you come from wealth. I still have that impression. Your family's well-off, and I bet you're not the first in line to be named Gideon."

He offered a small, stiff smile. "The fourth."

Not surprising.

"You live around here somewhere," I continued. "You have a private driver who takes you to work in the morning and wherever you need to go. You're a reliable man and probably stand by your commitments even when you shouldn't." I got a slight reaction to that. The corners of his eyes tightened. "You're an aggressive and instinctual lover, and you need to stay in control —or so you think. *I* think, if you found someone you trusted wholeheartedly, you'd enjoy letting your guard down and have another person take care of you, at least outside the bedroom. What else?" I drummed my fingers absently against the table. "This exploring thing... I don't know, I'm guessing social stigma and fear of not being accepted has kept you in the closet about being gay or bi. In old-school circles, it's still taboo to be different."

I wasn't cocky enough to believe I was right on the money,

but I was close... I could tell. He was back to avoiding eye contact, and his jaw ticked with tension. I sensed the restlessness in his posture.

"I also think you've successfully created a world of order and structure around yourself," I said, "and it isn't all it's cracked up to be."

That one earned me a sharp look.

"Without structure, my world falls apart," he said tightly. "I spent my childhood in and out of panic attacks, and it took me years to find ways to cope in our society. What you see today— every step I take, every word that comes out of my mouth—is due to structured training and confining myself. We speak figuratively about children learning to crawl before they can walk, but for me, there were approximately a dozen steps between crawling and walking."

I showed my palms to indicate I wasn't arguing with him— or doubting him, for that matter.

"I start out in a small box," he added. "Inch by inch, I expand it."

"I believe you, hon," I replied quickly. Because I didn't want him to think I didn't. He was clearly sensitive about this. "But then you also know that our arrangement—the way you designed it originally—never woulda given you what you wanted. Right? 'Cause you've expanded the box now. We're talking. We see each other. No one's wearing a mask, and we don't need the dark anymore."

His intense gaze flickered from one spot on my face to another as he processed what I'd said.

"In retrospect, yes," he conceded.

I nodded once. "I shook your structure. And you lived. It was uncomfortable for a moment, and you had to adjust, but we pulled through, didn't we? That's my only point—and you've done it your whole life. You've pushed yourself and created new boundaries." I gestured between us. "We're the same. You established a perimeter for our relationship, and then we reached a point where it wasn't enough. You said you felt alone when I wasn't participating."

He nodded, remembering. It'd been such a pivotal point.

"I'm obviously gonna do my best not to push you too hard," I went on. "But I think you're stronger than you appear to believe. I don't think you're obeying boundaries right now because you're not ready for more—I think it's something else. You've mentioned having commitments. Something about this—about us—is supposed to be purely physical."

"Well, yes." He cleared his throat and shifted in his seat. "A physical arrangement was the agreement I made with my fiancée. It was what she agreed to."

I stared at him, waiting, and I felt like we'd reached the stage where it was time he told me about this engagement of his. But maybe I was wrong? The lines were getting blurry, and I could possibly be getting ahead of myself. I just felt like we'd made such good progress...

But in the end, I was still a piece of ass he paid for.

I scratched my forehead, unsure of how to proceed.

"Your observational skills are a little too good," he said, glancing toward the booth across the narrow aisle. "I live two streets away. I do have a driver, and he's the only one who knows I'm attracted to men." He coughed a little and directed his gaze to the table. "Except for Claire, then. I told her a few months ago when we discussed marriage. I told her I couldn't go through with anything while I had these...thoughts and urges."

Claire.

I wanted to know about her as much as I wanted to forget her name.

Gideon sighed and scrubbed his hands over his face. "What if you're right? What if I won't be satisfied?"

A breath gusted out of me. I couldn't help but feel relieved that he was at least asking himself that question.

"That box I've lived in hasn't been expanded in years," he admitted. "I've grown comfortable, but at the same time..." He exhaled and sent a look skyward. "What was once necessary structure has started to feel like a prison."

Then he knew he had some thinking to do. Some decisions to make.

"There's one thing I gotta ask," I told him. "How does your fiancée agree to all this? You don't strike me as someone who's in an open relationship."

He waved me off absently, lost in thought. "We're not marrying for love. That helps."

"Uh..." I kinda needed him here in the moment to elaborate. "What are you marrying for?"

For having been so private—like a fucking vault—he seemed to have no issues spilling everything now. "We look good together on paper, and she has political aspirations." He paused. "My family is also becoming extinct, and she's promised me children."

Welp. That was that, then.

I averted my stare to another booth and cursed myself internally. I cursed that stupid, hopeless romantic in me.

To be honest, I never would've guessed Gideon's dream in life was to have kids.

"So, there are no brothers and sisters popping out heirs in your family," I concluded.

"Not even my parents did that. They tried for years, but I was their only child, and they had me late in life." He flicked me a quick glance. "They're dead."

"Oh. I'm sorry to hear that."

He shook his head minutely and gathered his napkin and the paper sleeves from his fries. "I'm the one who should apologize. I didn't mean for things to get heavy—or this personal. Now I'm uncomfortable."

I could tell, and there was no time to halt him before he rose from his seat and carried the tray over to the trash bins.

He was slamming his walls back into place, and I couldn't allow it. We didn't have to continue with the heavy; I bet he was overwhelmed too, but I didn't want him closing himself off.

On our way out of the restaurant, I asked him if there was a risk Claire or any of his neighbors could see him here.

He frowned in confusion. "Claire and I don't live together yet—she has her own place across the park—and I don't believe Mrs. Nelson is out walking her dog at this hour. Why?"

Well, then. I grinned and pulled him to me once we were outside, and I reached up to kiss him. "I wanted to steal a kiss, that's all."

He tested a small smile and kissed me chastely.

"Walk with me," I murmured. "Let's leave the heavy talk behind for a beat, and we'll just walk. We can call the driver whenever we want."

Even in the darkness of the street, the warmth seeping into his eyes was unmistakable.

"I'd like that," he responded quietly. "May I ask you more questions?"

"Of course." I was bold enough to grab his hand and link our fingers together, but he didn't seem to mind. "I'm an open book."

He glanced down at our hands as we reached the corner of Park Avenue, and he twisted his mouth upward slightly.

I was hooked on watching him process things.

"I'm curious about your job," he said. "You said you gave up being a sex worker two years ago?"

"Yeah."

"Did you have different personas?"

79

I quirked a brow.

"I'm wondering if you were always yourself with customers," he clarified. "Or if you pretended to be someone else."

Hmm. I studied him from the corner of my eye and wondered if he was asking for a specific reason. Like, if I was myself with *him*. If he was getting the real deal.

"Sometimes I added a layer, I guess you can say," I answered pensively. It felt important that I explained this properly to him, 'cause I didn't want him to misunderstand. "I've had clients who prefer boyish twinks, for instance—and clients who want to engage in conversation about their passions in life. So yeah, there's been some pretending involved. I mean, this one guy loved Russian literature, and I had to pretend to be interested in listenin' to him talk about it." I paused. "Then I quit. I walked away because it became lonely. I was a quick and temporary fix to most of these men. I was the scratch to their itch." I tightened my hold on Gideon's hand when he tensed up next to me. "In the two years I worked for Tina, I became good at reading people. Put me in a room with twenty men, and I'll point out the loneliest fucker in two minutes."

That was the pain in my former field. It was flooded with loneliness. Men who hid who they were and tried to tell themselves that a quick fuck with a whore would be enough for them.

"Fast-forward two years of slinging macchiatos and cheeseburgers," I continued. "I forgot about the pretending and the personas, to use your words—presumably somewhere between struggling to pay the bills and going nowhere—and then I met you." I cleared my throat, a little amused by how fucking naïve I'd been. "It didn't even occur to me to pretend with you, Gideon. I've been out of the game for too long. You talk about breaking rules? I've already broken several of my own."

"What rules?" he asked carefully.

I shrugged, even as my heart started pounding, and I went with honesty. "Don't get involved, for one. Don't get personally invested or attached. Don't fuck without protection."

He nodded slowly, and I kept facing forward and did my best to stay casual. I'd just admitted to him that I was getting attached to him, and I wasn't sure he interpreted it that way. I didn't even know if I wanted him to say he felt the same. It was a messy situation, one I couldn't afford to lose. Thousands of dollars and my future were at stake, so whether he would go on with his life after this, or he would like to explore something else with me, it had to wait.

"We've both broken rules, then," Gideon murmured.

"Mm."

I welcomed the silence that followed. I wasn't ready to hear anything, and he obviously had nothing to say.

It was for the best.

We kept walking in the New York night, hand in hand, talking a little, but saying nothing in particular.

"Nicky, we gotta discuss this new song of yours after tonight."

"No, we don't." I offered an innocent smile as Anthony rejoined us after getting a new microphone. We were supposed to rehearse at the church, but a Vigil service took precedence, so we'd opened up one of our rehearsal rooms at the academy tonight. The choir was here and warmed up, and then one of the microphones had acted up.

Anthony shot me an annoyed look before walking over to the platform in the back where the choir stood.

I knew what he wanted to say anyway. I wasn't having it.

My phone buzzed on the top of the piano. It was a message from Gideon.

I'm not a fan of you having a day off.

I smirked.

I wasn't a huge fan of it either. I missed him. It was fucking crazy how that man had gotten under my skin in just a month. But the outdoor concert was approaching, and my ass needed some recovery. Last night, Gideon had taken me for a walk in Hell's Kitchen. We walked a lot these days, actually—to chitchat, of all things—and I had expected what'd become our new normal. A walk and then, when we came home, some good fucking until we fell asleep. Instead, he'd taken me hard in a dark alleyway behind a bar, and I'd been too turned on to point out that he hadn't used enough lube.

I'd also been too turned on to ask for a break once we got back to the apartment. The man drove me bonkers and had revved up my sex drive to the max.

If I invited him down here—on a night I wasn't charging him—would he show up? I mean, if he had nothing to do... Maybe we could go out for a drink afterward. It sounded so normal in my head, and I wanted something normal with him.

Nothing ventured, nothing gained, right?

I texted him quickly.

If you have nothing better to do, I'm rehearsing with the choir at my brother's academy tonight. I'll buy you a drink when we're done if you're interested.

"Okay, from the start," Anthony announced. "We'll do Nicky's song after."

Finally.

So far, we'd only worked on it separately. I'd sent the choir the sheet music along with my notes earlier in the week, and Anthony and I had tinkered with it during our lunch breaks.

I hoped it made the set list for the concert. We had enough Christian songs, one of which we were practicing tonight.

Anthony was amazing as always, and he existed only for the music. He sang and played guitar, facing the choir, while I sat at the piano. And it happened to give me a view of the hallway outside the rehearsal studio, and I spotted Shawn through the window about halfway through the song.

The fuck was he doing here?

He removed his beanie and mittens and glanced through the window, in search of Anthony, but his gaze landed on me first.

I cocked a brow.

He rolled his eyes and kept searching until he found his ATM.

Without regard to what we were doing, Shawn opened the door and walked over to Anthony.

It made me livid in a flash of a second, and I let out a sharp whistle.

"Oi! You can wait." We were in the middle of the mother-fucking song, and Anthony was concentrating.

My brother obviously heard me, and he furrowed his brow at me before he looked over his shoulder and saw his boyfriend.

"I just need a second, asshole," Shawn spat at me.

"Why, because your first one's too loose?" I asked.

Anthony coughed.

Maria and a few others let out a collective spluttered laugh, and the song kinda died out when Anthony stopped playing.

I stopped playing too.

Shawn shot me a glare but made no further comment. He was dressed for a Friday night in the city, so I bet he was in a hurry. He squatted down in front of Anthony and turned on the charm, speaking too quietly for me to hear, though I already knew he was here to ask for cash. It was what he did, and my infuriating brother always gave it to him.

Or maybe not this time?

I tilted my head, not bothering to pretend to be subtle, and watched Anthony's body language. There was tension in his shoulders, but he spoke casually. Nothing casual about Shawn, though. He scowled at whatever Anthony had said.

My phone buzzed, and I dragged my gaze away to check it. A reply from Gideon.

I'd be a poor stalker if I announced my presence.

I grinned and typed back.

Well, if someone were to decide to stalk me, it's the second entrance where there's a sign for rehearsal studios. The door code is 7845, and I'm in the first room to the right. Stalkers are encouraged to take a seat in one of the chairs along the wall. Just in case.

If he did show up, I'd be somewhat surprised. He'd told me he wasn't comfortable with other people's spontaneity. He needed time to mentally prepare himself and go over all the steps and routes and risks. He'd also told me he believed it was the reason he couldn't cook, whereas he was great at baking bread. Baking was like math. There were perfect formulas to follow to achieve perfection. Cooking required a practiced touch and feeling, he'd said.

I had to admit I loved getting to know him. Bit by bit, he shared parts of himself during our walks, sometimes serious topics, but mostly easygoing stuff.

Learning about Claire was probably tougher on me than on him at this point. I'd found out she was a family friend—Gideon's cousin's family had a lake house next to Claire's family's "estate," and so on and so on, and just shoot me. She was perfect for him in the vision Gideon had created. A family life with heirs and lake houses and private jets. Blah.

Shawn stood up and marched for the exit, and I looked over at my brother in question. He just shook his head subtly, not wanting to get into it, and ordered everyone to focus and get back to work.

When he lost his politeness, which was rare, everyone heeled and listened.

It was a physical jab in the anxiety pump to hear Anthony snap at you because it happened practically never.

An hour later, we were all lost in the music again.

Anthony and I were both playing the guitar for this, and the song was fast enough for us to have worked up a sweat. I fucking loved it. We were in our element. We played, we sang, we stopped to make changes, and the choir was given freedom to be creative with the harmonies. Sometimes, it was the best way to create a song. To let it surface from a sea of improvised freedom.

We had Sylvia, an old classmate of Anthony's, playing synth next to Luiz on the drums, and she'd gotten a lot better at her new hobby since last time. It was Anthony who'd encouraged her to learn an instrument after her sister died, and she'd always loved the eighties...

"Sorry!" Tia exclaimed after mixing up the cues for the harmonies. I shook my head and made a quick circular motion, silently telling her to just jump in again, before I played the next lick. It was our favorite way to work, to keep going and going until we nailed the song.

Anthony hit the chorus again and sang of getting back up

and holding on tight because love was hard. And it was fucking supposed to be. I wanted to drill the lyrics into his skull.

The third verse was quiet, with focus on the synth and backup vocals, and it built up to the last chorus where I got some action too. I stepped forward to the microphone and joined in on the singing.

Anthony and I stood across from each other so we could communicate throughout the rehearsal, and when he nodded at my guitar and said, "After the third, I want more freestyle," I knew what to do.

We started the song all over again.

Everyone was fired up, and it was a rush to me. To Anthony too. To have this steady flow of energy traveling through us—it was why we loved playing.

I grinned and screwed my eyes shut as I missed a cue, but there was no time to think about it. Keep going, keep going. I jumped in again as soon as I could, and I blew out a heavy breath.

A beat later, I noticed a handful of friends in the choir glancing at the door, so I looked over too, and I smiled widely. *He came.* Gideon actually showed up. He looked a little ruffled in his very unruffled suit; my guess was that he was a bit over-whelmed, but he offered a small smile and sat down in one of the chairs below the window.

My eyes were still on him as I leaned toward the mic and sang backup for Anthony, and I prayed Gideon paid attention to the lyrics too. Then I backed off and dropped my gaze and delivered what I hoped was an impressive solo, short as it may be. It wasn't the kind of song to amaze, to be honest.

It would be kinda cool if he were amazed by me, though.

At around ten, everyone was starting to get tired and checking the clock on the wall a lot, so it was time to wind things down. Gideon had spent half an hour watching us rehearse the same song over and over, and that couldn't have been a blast. But he was here. He hadn't checked his phone a single time either.

"Only one rehearsal to go!" Maria exclaimed happily.

"We'll have two hours in the morning the same day as the concert too," Anthony replied, reaching for his towel to wipe his face.

I wiped my forehead on the sleeve of my Henley.

"Only two rehearsals to go!" Maria corrected jokingly.

The first rush of people was quick to say their goodbyes and wish everyone a happy weekend before ducking out, leaving Anthony and me with Maria, Luiz, Sylvia, and Nina. While Anthony huddled with most of them to shoot the shit, Maria and I went over the set list—what we had so far, anyway—so she could print it out for everyone for next time.

"So we're moving 'Testify' to the first section?" she asked, holding up her binder.

I nodded and tapped a finger to an empty slot. "Yeah, and this one goes from here to the last one."

During the event, we'd play five songs in three different time slots. Fifteen songs in total, with breaks in between for other acts. A local kids' comedian was coming, and there was some auction with the proceeds going to a shelter.

We had thirteen songs at this point. After checking with Anthony this week, we'd added "Stand by Me" to the last slot, and I was fairly certain he'd choose "Washed by the Water" as the fourteenth. It was one we'd performed with the choir before, so it wouldn't require a lot of practice.

"By the way, is there any news about Nashville?" Maria asked.

"Anthony would know that better than me," I replied. "I think we've shared all the info. You're in, right?"

"Of course! I'm not missing that." She bumped her hip to

mine, and I grinned. "We're gonna party it up in the South, papi."

"Fuck yeah."

Next spring, we had a gig at a rock festival outside Nashville, and we'd left it open to the choir to join us. We were an on-again, off-again band—or rather, a band with plenty of hiatuses —and it wasn't anything we put that much energy into. It was just fun to play here and there. This festival happened to be right up our alley, so Anthony had submitted a demo, and we'd been picked in the first selection, which was fucking cool if you asked me. But it wouldn't make us rich or anything. In fact, we were chartering a bus and staying at the cheapest hotel in the area, and those from the choir who wanted to join us had to pay for their own room and board.

Nine men and women from the choir had signed up, last I checked.

By the time Maria said it was time for her to hurry home, Anthony was alone with Luiz by the drums, and I could finally say hey to Gideon.

"See you next week, babe." I closed the door after Maria, then turned to the hottest man in the universe. "I don't wanna tiptoe around anything, so I'm just gonna come out and say it made me really fucking happy that you showed up."

Gideon had shared with me the countless hours he'd spent in front of the mirror perfecting "casual, polite, kind" smiles, and he wasn't bad at those. He blended in just fine. But when the smile warmed up his eyes, that was when I knew it was genuine. It was small, but it was there.

"I wanted to see you." He rose from his seat and smoothed down his suit jacket. "You're very talented."

"Thank you." I wanted to kiss him but figured that would be too much. "Did you dislike these lyrics too?"

I'd been right about the other song. Gideon hadn't liked it

because it hit too close to home. He just hadn't clarified further than that, so I remained in the dark. Was it about the settling for less than what he really wanted, for instance? Or was he feeling trapped?

"I didn't dislike them, no." It sounded like he'd phrased himself that way for a reason. Not disliking them didn't automatically translate to liking them.

"I wrote it for my brother." I reached out quickly and pretended to adjust the lapel on his suit. "But if you took something from it, I'd call it a bonus."

Gideon peered down at his chest, then lifted a brow at me and smirked faintly. "I can pick up *some* subtle cues, you know."

"Good!" I let out a laugh.

"I know you don't want me to hide who I am," he murmured.

My humor faded, and I shook my head. "No, I don't." I spotted Luiz and Anthony coming closer, so I looked over at them. "Good job today, man." I held out my fist.

Luiz bumped it with his own. "You too. See ya Wednesday?"

"Definitely." I was gonna go over some advice with him then because he wanted to advance as a drummer.

Once he had left, I could sense that Gideon's focus was on Anthony, and I wanted to show him he could trust me to make a possibly awkward moment as painless as it could be. Work was mixing with family, and when work was sex work, it could be uncomfortable for anyone, with or without a diagnosis.

"Gideon, this is my brother Anthony. Anthony, Gideon," I said. "We're gonna go grab a beer. You wanna come with?"

I knew he'd say no.

"Nice to meet you." Anthony shook Gideon's hand firmly before addressing me. "Nah, I gotta be up early, but you have fun."

He was a pro. He'd save his questions for later. And he really did have to be up early.

After grabbing our jackets, we made our way outside, and Anthony activated the alarm before locking up.

"I guess I'll see you at Nonna's?" he asked, pocketing his keys.

"Always. But I'll call you tomorrow to bug you with worries and so on." I felt like a mothering fretter around my brother at times, but it was what it was. I wanted him happy and cared for.

"Can't wait." He offered a wry smirk, even though I knew he appreciated the concern as much as it bugged him. At least on the topic of his love life.

Anthony veered right with a two-finger wave, aiming for the parking lot next to the building, and Gideon gestured toward the street for me, where my gaze landed on a car that didn't belong in this area. And Park Slope was *nice*.

Just not Bentley SUV with a private driver nice.

"Madonn', Daddy, this is a $200,000 car." I drew a finger along the glossy black exterior as Gideon opened the door for me.

"Do you have an interest in cars?" He cocked his head, looking like he hadn't expected me to have such a hobby.

And I didn't. I shook my head and slid into the car, offering a nod of greeting to the driver—who offered absolutely nothing in return. "My pop had his own body shop before he retired," I answered. "He lives and breathes cars. I used to run around down there all the time as a kid."

"Back to Manhattan, sir?" the driver asked.

Gideon looked to me in question. "Where would you like to go?"

I knew just the place, and I was suddenly antsy to show Gideon a little about my life. I gave the driver the address to

Sueños, a small bar in Williamsburg where I'd had my first legal shot of tequila after turning twenty-one.

Gideon wouldn't feel overly overwhelmed there. It was a lively place, but the booths were designed as little pockets with cabana themes that provided a semblance of privacy. Plus, it was gay-friendly, and I knew the owners.

"You're about to discover why my Spanish is better than my Italian," I joked.

The other day, he had quizzed me about my ancestry after I'd called him papi. Like so many others in the Northeast, I was Irish and Italian, though the only stereotypically Irish thing about me was the color of my eyes. They were from Ma's side, and she hadn't been solely Irish herself. The Italian dominated. But growing up in a Latin neighborhood had left its marks, and I was a professional language butcher, mixing Italian, English, Spanish, and slang. More so than Anthony, who'd done the adult thing and polished his skills to be able to say he was fluent in three languages. Me? Half the time, I didn't know what was what.

When I told Gideon this, I thought he'd find it funny. Instead, he pursed his lips and eyed me like he'd just solved a math problem.

"You always place your brother a little higher than your-self," he noted. "He's better at languages, at singing, at playing the piano, he's higher educated, he's more business-minded, et cetera."

Damn. Did I do that? I squinted at nothing and scratched my ear.

"I hadn't thought of that. It's not a way to put myself down, though," I replied. "If you want a good Sunday dinner and our grandmother's not around, you want me, not Anthony. I'm better with the guitar, and I think I'm scrappier than he is. He's calmer and more careful. I'm impulsive and don't mind taking some risks."

He chuckled. "You list traits about yourself that I usually abhor and do anything to stay away from, and yet..." He released a breath and shook his head. "You're all I can think of, Nicky."

There was no stopping the shit-eating grin on my mug.

I was fairly certain it was the first time he'd called me by my name, too. Or nickname.

"Nicky," he repeated to himself. "Normally, I don't even like nicknames."

"Fuck normal, baby. I like that I stand out." I grabbed his hand and kissed the top of it, then linked our fingers together and rested them on the narrow seat between us. "Who doesn't wanna be memorable, right?"

"Memorable... That's an understatement." He smiled wryly. "You're very...colorful."

Both good and bad, I assumed. I bet I shook up his gray existence, but it didn't take a whole lot to do that. He came from a typically WASP-y line of golfers, investors, and yacht club members. I knew enough about him that it wouldn't take more than a Google search to find out exactly who he was, and the reason I hadn't done that was because I didn't wanna see just how different we were. Too different wasn't a positive thing. Too different was frightening in Gideon's world.

I was his spice.

The scratch to his itch...

Fucking hell.

CHAPTER 7

Sueños, the place where dreams didn't come true, but you could have a good fucking time. Latin remixes of pop songs blared out of the speakers as usual, and the walls screamed of Mexico, Puerto Rico, and the Caribbean with murals painted by Camila.

"Nicky! Don't even try to sit down before you've said hey!" Valeria hollered from the bar. "Mama! Nicky's hea'!"

I grinned and turned to Gideon. "Grab us a booth. I'll be there in a minute—unless you want me to introduce you to Camila and her four loud daughters."

He widened his eyes. "I'll pass."

Thought so. I could tell he was already tense, and we'd just gotten here. But no matter how small the bar was, it was probably packed by his standards. To me, a place wasn't packed until you could smell at least twenty different perfumes. To him, it was when the booths were filled.

I smacked a kiss to his jaw, then made my way to the bar, where I elbowed myself in between two men.

"Hey, darlin'." I reached over the bar and kissed Valeria's cheek just as her mother appeared from the back.

Camila and her girls had been a big part of my teenage years. I'd gone to school with the youngest, Isabella, who was the coolest goth chick in Brooklyn, but it was safer to introduce them to Gideon one at a time.

"Nicky, what's this I hear about you leavin' Brooklyn?" Camila asked, looking offended.

"Don't listen to gossip!" I didn't know who to blame. Anthony wasn't one to spread that shit around. "It's two months, and then I'll probably be crashing at Anthony's again."

"Uh-huh." She leaned forward, and I dutifully kissed her cheek too. "Don't tell your abuela. You'd break her heart."

"Ay, with the drama," I laughed. "If you know, I'm shocked she doesn't."

"Whas'at supposed to mean?" she hollered.

"Nothin'!" I insisted. "Can I get some service? I brought a hot date."

I looked behind me and—oh man. I kinda adored him. He'd found a booth, and he was currently wiping down the table with a disinfectant wipe.

"The Suit cleaning the table?" Valeria asked. "Sofia just wiped them down."

I shrugged. I wasn't getting into it with them. "Anyway." I twirled a finger.

Camila gave her daughter's shoulder a squeeze. "I'll be in the office. Don't be a stranger, Nicky."

Isabella appeared next, and we bumped fists as Valeria delegated my drink order to her sister, which suited me just fine. Valeria could move on to the other patrons and water down their drinks while Isabella gave me doubles of everything.

I ordered a gin and tonic, a beer, a glass of red, and a Blue Lagoon for some variety.

"Didju hear about Maxine from school?" she asked, pouring Gideon's wine.

I nodded grimly. "Nonna told me. I hope she gets full custody and that her two-bit fucker—" I flipped my fingers under my chin "—goes back to Rikers."

"Seriously." She arranged all four drinks on a tray and asked if I wanted to open a tab.

"Nah. I don't think we'll be here that long." I handed over my card and grabbed the tray.

"Ay. Before you saunter off." She swiped my card with one hand and poured two shots of tequila with the other, and I chuckled and shook my head.

I took one of the little glasses and threw it back, hissing at the burn in my throat.

She swallowed her shot without making a single grimace—unless one counted her smirk.

I pocketed my card. "Bitch. Later."

"Later, hoodrat." She blew me a kiss.

Lifting the tray over my head, I started making my way through the crowd, and I nodded and hollered hellos to a handful of people I knew. Ed Sheeran's "South of the Border" began playing as I emerged in front of the little booth Gideon had picked, and I bobbed my head to the beat and spun my imaginary turntables. My Friday had gone from ice cream sundae at the keyboard in a quiet apartment to having drinks at one of my favorite bars with the man of my fantasies. Safe to say, I was in a good mood.

"Hey there, gorgeous. Wine for you, beer for me, and two extras because one is never enough." I slid in next to him rather than across from him. It was a tight fit, but no matter. This was the place to be for privacy and lewd behavior under the table.

Best part of the Caribbean theme? The mosquito netting that could be closed like a curtain, effectively shutting out the world. Here, it was just the two of us and bamboo. Or whatever wood imitation the booth was built from.

"It's very loud here," Gideon said. "I like the net, though. But we can still see through it."

"It used to be regular fabric, but then Camila caught a bunch of fuckers doing blow in public, so... This is why we can't have nice things." I took a swig of my beer and squeezed his thigh.

"I'm sorry, I'm processing," he informed me. "My mind is spinning with impressions and you doing...things."

"What things?" Had I gone too far? Maybe this was a bad idea. We could always go back to the apartment.

"Just the way you act." He shifted the wineglass closer to him and traced a finger along the stem. "You're carefree and appear to have countless friends. Your behavior. Your laughter, your banter, how you made that Italian gesture—with your fingers under your chin?—and how easily you maneuvered yourself through the crowd with four drinks. This is nothing to you."

"Hon, I've been working in restaurants on and off since I was fourteen," I explained patiently.

"That's only one thing. I understand you've had practice," he said. Then he shook his head, visibly frustrated. "This isn't me, Nicky. Your life is vibrant. You speak with your entire body, whereas I was raised not to stand out in a crowd because that's embarrassing. How can I ever make a lasting impression in your life?"

Oh, fuck me. Was that something he aimed for? Because he'd already succeeded.

"The most colorful item in my life is a red tie that I wear at Christmas," he finished.

"I have plenty of color in my life," I agreed. "That's why I'm not looking for color." I waited until he made eye contact, and the uncertainty in his eyes nearly did me in. "Color can easily be translated into madness. There's rarely a dull moment, no sitting still, very little stability, and no structure. And getting to know you has made me realize that's what I need more of." I sat up straighter so I could drape an arm along the back of the booth, and I rubbed his neck gently. "But should we really be talking about this, papito? As far as I know, we part ways in a month, and you go off to marry a woman who can have your kids."

I needed to protect myself more than ever. Gideon was dangerous as he was, and if he was having doubts and getting attached too, it would possibly break me. 'Cause I knew I wouldn't have the strength to walk away first.

And if there was one thing I'd learned from my years as a sex worker, it was that the husband never left the wife.

Gideon stared at his wineglass before bringing it to his lips and taking a big swallow of it. "Have you wondered... Good grief, that's awful wine."

I exhaled a laugh, my stomach tightening in anticipation of what he was gonna ask.

"If the circumstances were different..." He cleared his throat. "Would you be interested—I mean, have you considered—"

"Yeah. You?"

He swallowed and nodded minutely.

Fuck. My heart pounded against my rib cage.

For a moment, his façade shattered. He looked crestfallen and utterly lost. "I truly want a family. My own family spent decades building New York and forgot that families need building too. I'd walk away from everything they created for something bigger—a wife, or...you know, to come home to, and kids—people who are simply there."

Then there was fuck-all I could do. My family meant the world to me, so it was impossible not to empathize with his wistfulness. At the same time, it hurt. It was the one thing I wouldn't be able to give him, and it was clearly a deal-breaker.

"A family is a wonderful thing to be a part of." I had to show him I understood him. "I get it."

He nodded slowly and reached for the gin and tonic. "I always wanted a brother. My parents were loving and more affectionate than the rest of our family, but it still resulted in many lonely evenings. My father worked too much, and my mother was often away planning some benefit." He took a tentative sip of the gin and tonic, then a bigger swig. It must've received a better grade than the wine. "What about you? You're still so young, but have you thought about children and such?"

"Not really." I scratched his scalp at the back of his neck the way he liked. "I mean, don't get me wrong. I love kids. Love working with them, but no one's gonna let me adopt. I don't have the financial stability for that. I don't even have a home." I tried to lighten the tension with a chuckle, but I wasn't sure it worked. "In short, it's a conversation for once I have a place of my own, once I've gone into business with Anthony and we've expanded the academy, and once I'm in a committed relationship."

He inclined his head. "That makes sense." He closed his eyes as I kept weaving my fingers through his hair.

Why did our little outings always end up with the heaviest topics? Couldn't I just enjoy one evening out where I pretended we were on a date? Jeesh.

I drained half my beer and scrambled for something easier to talk about.

I guess since he and I definitely weren't happening, I might as well ask who he really was. His family spending decades building New York gave a hint or two.

"So, I take it you're from one of the real estate families that built the city," I said.

He hummed. "Are you asking for my last name?"

"Yeah, I reckon I am."

"Grant."

Holy shit. Gideon Grant IV. His last name appeared on skyscrapers—or at least two—and he fucking owned the building I was currently staying in. Funnily enough, they owned a shit-load of property here in Brooklyn, too. They'd been part of the transformation of Williamsburg in the nineties, when artists and spoiled rich kids replaced a lot of the guidos and micks such as myself.

"I'm picturing you bored out of your mind in some skyscraper boardroom day in and day out."

The corners of his mouth twisted up. "You're not far off. I have a right-hand man who functions as my filter and barrier, and somehow, I still end up in several meetings a day—and God knows with how many final approvals and signatures. Hardly what one might call an inspiring job." He furrowed his brow but didn't open his eyes. "If my cousins and nephew offered to buy me out, I'd probably consider it."

So how the fuck did he think he was gonna find satisfaction in the vision of his own future? Right now, there was a door he could walk out of. Once he got married and his wife had squeezed out a couple kids, the same door would be locked and bolted, and if he wanted to escape, he'd have to join the sorry band of married closet cases who sought out sex workers on the sly.

"Let's talk about something else," I suggested. "I told Camila and her girls that you're my hot date, so start acting like you might score tonight."

He grinned a little at that and cracked one eye open at me.

"Are you telling me there's a chance you might invite me to your place?"

I leaned in and kissed him softly. "Definitely."

He hummed and kissed me back. "I'm all yours until six AM. That's when I have to walk Chester."

"Chester."

"My dog."

I grinned into another kiss. "Of fucking course his name is Chester. Is it a golden retriever or a Schnauzer?"

He huffed and pulled away from me, and he stuck a hand inside the inner pocket of his suit. "I'm glad not everything about me is predictable, Mr. Profiler." He pulled out his phone. "Chester is a Havershire, a mix between Yorkshire terrier and Havanese."

Weren't they tiny?

Gideon's screen flashed to life, and there it was. The background picture was of a dog, but he didn't stay there. He went to his photo album instead and clicked on another photo.

What a cute fur ball. Definitely a lap dog. Its white-and-brown coat pointed in every direction, and dirt and leaves were stuck to his legs. The soft-looking ears let me know Gideon didn't mess around with grooming. I bet he took the dog to some overpriced dog stylist.

"We have a dog walker in my building who takes him out a couple times every day, but I try to make it home for mornings and evenings," he murmured, swiping to another picture. "His favorite pastimes are making a complete mess of himself in the park, cuddling up on my lap when I read, and listening to my daily work ramblings. Or so I hope. Otherwise, I'm a horrible owner."

I shifted my gaze to Gideon's face instead. It was the first time I could see him with a kid. He truly loved that dog, and I supposed it made sense. I'd read in one of the books I'd borrowed that autistic people sometimes connected easier with children and pets than other adults.

"I've been thinking about adopting a brother for him," Gideon admitted. He was lost in his own photo album, going from one picture to another. It seemed the whole album was filled with images of Chester. "It would have to be one who got along with Chester, though. He's very active when we're outside, but the minute we come home, he wants to sleep or take it easy on my lap." He grinned fondly. "Sometimes he'll nip at the bottom of my pants and run toward the living room or the library. It's his way of telling me I've been on my feet for too long."

Cazzo, I was gonna fall for this fucker before our arrangement was over.

I finished my beer, torn between jumping his bones and running away to hide, because I knew I wasn't gonna win this round. I wouldn't be able to stop myself from handing over my heart on a goddamn platter.

Hell, I wasn't strong enough to run away either.

Screw it all. I leaned in again and kissed his jaw. "Come home with me, papi. I need your big fat cock."

Funny how quickly he lost interest in his phone. "Okay. Let me pay for the drinks first."

"Already took care of it."

"Oh." He frowned for a beat before his eyes heated up with some indecent idea. "Then let me treat you to something else before we go back to your place."

The dirtier, the better.

———

Half an hour later, Gideon's driver pulled up in front of an adult store back in Manhattan, and I was beginning to wonder if this was the reason only the driver—aside from Claire—knew of Gideon's sexuality. Because Gideon had simply said "West Village," and the driver had known exactly what that meant.

So Gideon had been here before.

Long gone were the seedy places with boarded-shut windows and back alleys. In the heart of an LGBTQ neighborhood, this store was brightly lit and showcasing its services right in the window alongside boxed sex toys, stacks of movies, and kinky outfits. They had six private booths, two double suites, whatever that meant, a glory hole, and a theater that seated eighteen guests.

"We won't be long. Perhaps thirty minutes," Gideon told his driver.

Once we were on the curb and Gideon had closed the door, he turned to me and unzipped my jacket. There was a new air to him; he was assertive and in charge of the situation.

"Are you up for some role-playing?" he asked.

"Sh-yeah." I blinked up at him, instantly intrigued and turned on. "You've been here before."

He inclined his head. "It's been my once-a-year indulgence the past ten years."

Hot damn. "What do you do when you come here?"

He raked his teeth across his bottom lip and smirked a little. "Not much. I rent a booth and masturbate with the door ajar. People enjoy watching."

"And you like being watched." I stepped closer and slid a hand up his chest. "You're an exhibitionist."

It was funny to me that he could hesitate to go into a grocery store without a shopping list, but he had no issues being in control as soon as it was about sex. That part of him wasn't merely confident; it was utterly fucking shameless.

"Neurotypical humans take sex too seriously," he said. "I'm not an exhibitionist so much as I enjoy making people nervous.

It turns me on to see them out of their element. To see them hesitate and wonder what's protocol."

My eyebrows went up, and...well, so did my cock.

This was his alternate universe. A place where he was the assertive norm and everyone else was scrambling, like he felt he did in society, in his everyday life.

He cupped my jaw and brushed a thumb over my barely there scruff. I'd shaved yesterday. "You can pass for twenty," he murmured. "Sweet boy."

Jesus.

His raw masculinity and power pushed me straight into a subservient mind-set.

"Just follow my lead, okay? The trick is to take it slowly at first so everyone who doesn't want to take part can leave."

Um. Everyone? Take part?

Rather than taking my hand or something, he slipped a hand to the back of my neck and ushered me into the store, which was surprisingly small. Considering all they bragged about in the window, I'd expected something bigger. But there were arrows on the floor leading to the back, so I guessed all the booths were in another section, separated from the store.

Gideon guided me straight up to the register, where a guy my age was flipping through a catalogue with a bunch of leather outfits. He glanced up and straightened as he spotted Gideon.

"How can I help you, sir?"

Oh, step off, bitch. Not in any way you're hoping for.

He reminded me of Shawn.

Gideon tightened his grip on my neck a little and patted my chest. "I'm here as moral support to my son who's too shy to pick out some sex toys to experiment with."

Madonna fucking mia...what?!

Heat exploded within me, and I blushed like a fucking kid. It felt like my cheeks were suddenly on fire. My stare could not drop to the floor any faster, though not fast enough for me to miss the shock on the guy's face.

"It took me forever to drag it out of him," Gideon went on. "So I'd like to nip this in the bud and get it over with. Any recommendations?"

I didn't know what was worse, the fact that two couples nearby had clearly overheard Gideon, or that I was getting off on it. Despite the mortification...fuck it, no one turned me on like this man.

The guy behind the counter stuttered a quick direction to the vibrators, and I felt his stare burning a hole in the back of my skull as Gideon ushered me toward the rear of the store section.

The half-dozen men in the shop weren't hiding their curiosity for shit.

"Go on, then," Gideon said. "Pick out a vibrator."

I gulped and reverted to some clueless teenager, and I stepped forward and glanced at the wall of silicone dicks. Dildos next to vibrators of all shapes and, um, species. If I wanted to get probed by an alien dick, this store had me covered.

I'd owned a single sex toy in my life, a J-shaped prostate massager, though I'd been around plenty of other toys provided by former clients.

"It's past midnight, son. Pick up the pace a bit."

Fuck me.

I swallowed and grabbed the first prostate massager I could find. "Uh, this one?"

"I'll go grab a basket." He left me. He fucking left. And I stared after him, only to spot everyone who was having trouble minding their own business. Except, this was what Gideon wanted. He wanted an audience.

Christ, so did I. I wanted to see how far he'd take it, and the other men sure as hell didn't seem to mind either. Unless it was a coincidence they were suddenly checking out toys and movies that were closer to where I was standing.

I heard Gideon speak to someone, presumably the guy at the register, but I couldn't make out the words.

I turned back to the vibrator selection and gave it more than a cursory glance this time.

If this was gonna turn into a shopping spree, I could think of a toy or two to keep after Gideon moved on and married a woman. I'd need a dick that felt and looked like his, 'cause it wasn't a gay pity party until there was miserable masturbation involved.

I'd just grabbed an eight-inch dildo when Gideon returned with the guy from before.

"This young man offered to assist us," Gideon told me. "He'll write down what we put in the basket, and then we can open the boxes if needed."

Fuck me twice.

Okay, so that guy was just gonna stand there with his little notepad and the basket at his feet. And stare at us.

He didn't look so uncomfortable anymore. Quite the fucking opposite.

"Pretend I'm not here," he said.

Uh-huh.

"What've you got there, boy?" Gideon grabbed the boxed-up dildo from me and smirked a little. "You and your mother have the same taste."

Just when I thought my face couldn't turn redder.

I exhaled unsteadily and tried to say something, to move my goddamn feet, to do *anything*, but I was rooted in place. I was waiting for instructions. I was watching him like I watched porn.

Who was this filthy god?

"You'll need some type of lube if you're going to fit this one inside you, yes?"

I managed to nod, and I crept closer to his body as if he were going to protect me from himself. It couldn't be normal to sneak toward the danger, but damn if his danger wasn't making me hard.

He smiled down at me. "Have you gone mute?"

"N-no." I flushed and kicked myself mentally. Time to get my shit together. "It's just embarrassing, Dad."

"Nonsense. There's nothing embarrassing about exploring yourself." He dropped the dildo and the massager into the basket on the floor, then gestured toward the lube section. "Come on. Let's find you a bottle of lube."

I followed obediently and did my best to block out everyone else. How ironic, I'd been on his ass the first week about wanting to participate more, and now I'd lost my marbles.

"Wait. These look like fun, don't they?" He stopped at a display with cock rings. "They're supposed to make you last longer. Is that a problem you have?"

"Um. Maybe? I don't know. Sometimes I come fast." Like when he fucked me mercilessly and whispered what a dirty boy I was.

It didn't take much around this man, what could I say.

"It's nothing to worry about. I came fast at your age too." He draped an arm around my shoulders and pulled me to him. "What do you think? You want to try one of these?"

I eyed the black silicone ring inside its little plastic wrap, and I nodded. I remembered enjoying those before. "Could be fun, I guess."

He kissed my temple and held up the cock ring. "We'll take one of these, Steven." Then he started unwrapping it. "Unzip your pants, son. We don't know if it fits. There are three different sizes."

Oh my God.

"Here?" I squeaked.

Squeaked. Like a child.

He furrowed his brow, confused. "What's the problem? We're twenty feet away from men who are watching porn and getting each other off—we're surrounded by toys and dog collars. Do you think anyone's going to be offended if you try out a cock ring?"

Doctors performed surgeries in an OR; that didn't mean they would whip out their scalpels in the hospital cafeteria! *Gah.* But I didn't say that. Instead, I undid my jeans and gave up on trying to slow down my pulse.

"See, this is why I came with you tonight," he said. "If I left you in charge, you'd get nothing done." He took over for me, quickly pushing down my pants halfway across my ass, then the boxer briefs enough to reveal my hard-on. "Someone's excited already."

The mortification flooded me, reaching new levels, but so did the excitement. His detached, no-nonsense behavior was gonna be the death of me.

"Oh my God, Dad," I mumbled breathily. He rolled the tight silicone ring onto my cock and gave me a couple quick strokes.

"There," he murmured, straightening. His fingers remained on my cock, and he slowed down his movements. "It looks pleasurable."

I nodded jerkily, trying not to push into his hand. "So good."

"Lube's still missing, though. Follow me."

It was mere steps away, a few feet, and he made no indication that he wanted me to pull up my pants again.

He read the labels for a moment, then held up a bottle to Steven, who jotted something down. I wasn't paying attention to him. All I saw was Gideon opening the bottle of...liquid coconut oil.

"It's organic," he mentioned. "And edible." Then he gestured toward the door in the back. "Go pick a booth. You'll want to try it all out before we go home."

At this point, my default response to everything was *Oh my God.*

Me and my scarlet fucking face hightailed it toward the back of the store, where I wasn't one hundred percent sure we'd actually get more privacy. And I wasn't sure I cared.

Absently tugging my shirt over my cock, I stared down the hallway of booths and swallowed hard. One so-called twin booth was available, and I peered inside. There was a love seat, a flat screen, a wastebasket, and a condom dispenser. The room reeked of disinfectants, which beat the alternative.

I hung my jacket on a knob on the back of the door.

At least the place felt clean. The love seat was of some latex material. Not very comfortable against your skin, but easy to scrub down. And somehow, I knew that'd been a factor when Gideon was looking for a place like this.

He joined me shortly after, along with the basket, and he left the door ajar.

He shrugged off his coat too and hung it on the door. "All right. Push down your pants a bit more and bend over the sofa."

"Why?" I asked warily. "I can do this at home, Dad. This isn't normal."

"Neither is you sneaking around when I'm taking a shower," he replied without missing a beat. Then he snapped his fingers and pointed to the love seat. "Stop pretending you don't want me to help you."

Oh my God.

I dropped my gaze to the floor as two men appeared in the

doorway, and I did as told. Then Gideon changed his mind and instructed me to kneel on the love seat instead. So I did.

"I found a plug I thought you might enjoy," he mentioned. "I assume that's what you're looking for when you watch me in the shower. You want to be filled."

I squeezed my eyes shut and gasped when he drew a wet finger between my ass cheeks.

"Don't you have anything to say for yourself?" he asked.

Yeah. Please fuck me hard, Dad.

"I'm sorry?" I managed to get out. Fucking hell, that felt good. He'd coated his fingers and what I guessed was the butt plug in lube—a lot of it—and he was gliding the tip around my opening. But I preferred his fingers.

"You should be," he muttered. He drew a shudder from me when he pushed a lone finger inside. His middle finger. His long, perfect, slender middle finger. "You've created quite the problem for me, my boy. I might even call you a tease."

I moaned and gave up on the charade. Or rather, I couldn't pretend I wasn't aching for him any longer.

"Can I try the plug, Dad?" I begged. Because I needed something inside me right fucking now.

"So eager. Sure." He opened the bottle of lube again, and I snuck a quick peek toward the doorway. Holy shit. Three men now, and one was stroking himself.

The second Gideon began pushing the plug inside me, I realized there was something different about it. The ones I'd tried before had been smooth. This one was ribbed or had some kind of texture that made me feel like I was being fucked by the veiniest cock on the planet. Madonn', I was glad we were bringing it home with us. The silicone protrusions rubbed me from within and turned me into a hypersensitive head case.

"You're being a tease again, boy." He fucked me with the

plug in the slowest of strokes, letting me feel every ridge. "What else do you want in your bottom?"

That feverish heat made a swift return to my face. "Um."

Why couldn't I just say it? I'd never had any issues begging for his cock.

"Now you're shy?" The wry amusement in his voice pushed at my mind-set. It made me feel smaller in a strange way. Then he forced the plug all the way in and smacked my ass.

"*Hnngh.*" I failed to withhold a groan.

He eased away. "Get on your knees next to me." He reappeared and sat down on the love seat, leaving the spot closest to the door available. "It's time you tasted a big, proper cock. Not whatever it is you're doing when you're out with your little friends."

Fuck yes.

I scrambled into position while he unzipped his pants, and I knew exactly what the men in the doorway saw with my back to them. I bet Gideon knew too.

He didn't tell me what to do beyond what he'd already said. Instead, he released his cock from his boxer briefs, cupped the back of my neck, and pulled me down to him.

My mouth watered, and I took him as deeply as I could.

"This is what you want, isn't it?" he murmured. "My cock."

I nodded and swirled my tongue around him.

He hummed and slid his hand down to my ass, and he kneaded one cheek, spreading them both, giving our audience a show.

"That's good." He released a breath and moved his fingers into my hair. "Keep going. Oh, that's so good."

He tensed up a little as I sucked him harder.

I wasn't sure if I was doing this for him or for me, to be honest, because I'd grown seriously addicted to his long and thick cock.

"I'll give you ten seconds," he told me. "If you don't confess where you want your father's cock by then, I will zip up and take you home."

With those words and that ultimatum, I only needed two seconds.

"In my ass, Dad," I panted. I gripped his cock and stroked it quickly, and I flicked the tip of my tongue over the head. "I want you to fuck me."

He combed his fingers through my hair. "Mmm, wasn't so hard, was it?"

I gasped as a sharp sting radiated from the back of my head when he pulled me back.

"Daddy's going to make your dreams come true," he whispered against my cheek. Behind my back, he twisted the plug in my ass and slowly pulled it out. "I'll fill my boy's little bottom with so much come that it'll run down your legs later."

I whimpered, and my chest heaved with my next breath. I couldn't believe his filthy mouth—this was what winning the dirtiest lottery on the planet felt like. Whatever he wanted, he could have. I'd even get on my knees and beg him to take it.

On my knees was how he wanted me, too. With my hands grabbing the back of the sofa, I pushed my ass out for him while he stood behind me and lubed up his cock.

Then he gave my ass a solid smack, and all I did was moan something incoherent.

"You greedy little whore," he murmured. "I want you this desperate for me at all times."

"Yes, sir," I groaned. "Whenever you want."

He shifted one hand to my hip and used the other to guide his cock to my ass, and there was no warning. He sank into me in one slow, fluid thrust.

His exhale rocked me to my core. It was filled with pleasure and relief, and I wanted to make him feel that way forever.

He just fucking owned me. He fucked me, and he owned me. With a forceful grip on my hips, he drove his cock in and out of me and created the sexiest sounds whenever his pelvis hit my flesh.

Moans filled the air, and not all of them belonged to Daddy and me.

It made me wanna roll around in the attention we were given. I groaned pleadingly and arched my back, and I started stroking myself off. Sweat beaded over my skin. My breath turned shallow. And the rhythm fucked my brain. It was out of this world. Push, pull, Gideon's grunt, push, pull, Gideon's groan, push, pull, Gideon smacking my ass again.

"Harder, Daddy," I begged. Oh fuck, oh fuck, oh fuck. He felt fucking incredible, and he was hitting all the right places. "Fuck me harder."

He tightened his grip and slammed into me, and I cried out as pleasure and pain washed over me in a heated rush.

"Now that you've demonstrated what a needy slut you are," he grunted, "don't think for a second I won't come into your room at night."

I moaned and glanced at him over my shoulder, and I made sure to meet every single thrust. "I'll leave the door open every night."

"That's my good boy," he murmured, out of breath. "You'll keep me satisfied, won't you?"

I nodded quickly and whimpered. I was getting so close. I felt all feverish and desperate, and this fucking had to continue when we got home. There was no getting enough of him.

When he told me to come for him, to come for Daddy, I didn't make a single sound. I couldn't. I was too far gone in some delirious state where only he and I existed, and I could only obey. I let the euphoria grab ahold of me and sweep me the fuck away.

I just breathed and moved with the rhythm he controlled. Push, pull, push, pull. And the orgasm took over. Ropes of come shot from my cock, and I vaguely heard his breathing change. Quickly thereafter, his thrusts changed too. He fucked me harder once, twice, three more times before he rammed in and jerked inside me.

I was ready to collapse.

Oh my God.

I dropped my chin to my chest and waited for my heart to slow down.

Gideon brushed a sweet kiss between my shoulder blades, then carefully withdrew his cock.

I swallowed dryly.

Goose bumps rose all over me, and I couldn't stop shivering.

At the sound of a door clicking shut, I managed to open my eyes and look toward—oh, he'd closed it. I was glad, to be honest. The aftermath was private.

"You make me speechless sometimes, Nicky." He helped me off the love seat and gathered me in his arms, where he cupped my face and kissed me softly. "Let's get cleaned up so we can get out of here. I want us under the covers as soon as possible."

I shuddered some more, and I nodded. "Sounds perfect. But that...Jesus Christ..."

He smirked faintly. "You enjoyed it, yes?"

I widened my eyes and laughed shakily. "Understatement of the year."

"Good." He touched my cheek briefly. "Me too."

CHAPTER 8

The closer we got to the end of our arrangement, the more frequently our routine changed. I'd thought we'd established something that worked for us when we began our nightly dates with a walk and some chatting, and then we'd go back to my place and fuck and sleep, fuck and sleep, fuck and sleep.

Now we'd entered the week of my outdoor concert and the last two weeks of my companionship with Gideon, and he was all over the place. He showed up frustrated, he was forgetful and bringing up "chitchat" topics we'd already covered, sometimes he wandered off in his own world and didn't hear a word of what I was saying, and he struggled to get comfortable to sleep.

The last two nights, he hadn't gotten off, and he'd thought he'd distracted me from noticing by focusing solely on me and drawing as many orgasms out of me as he could.

Trust, I was still noticing, but I was trying to mind my own business when it seemed too personal. After all, I was who I was. Temporary in his life. Bought and paid for. I assumed he brought his problems to Claire or someone else, and I wasn't at all jealous about that, and that was two lies in one little thought. Impressive. For one, I fucking knew he didn't have anyone to talk to, and we could skip the "for two."

I scratched my forehead and then checked the time on my phone.

Three minutes past ten. I was waiting for him outside my building, and it was good walking weather. Not too cold, which it had been the past few nights, and the sun had been shining all day.

It occurred to me yesterday that I'd never seen Gideon in the light of day.

These past several weeks, I hadn't come to life until the sun went down, whether I was meeting with Gideon—it was mostly him—or I was having dinner with Anthony or catching a drink with Ruby and Chris.

Where *was* he?

I peered up and down the street.

His punctuality had spoiled me. He'd been late a single time, and he'd texted beforehand.

I was contemplating sending him a message when my phone rang, and it couldn't be him. He didn't like talking on the phone.

It was Anthony.

"Sup?" I answered.

"Oh. Hey. It's after ten, so I thought I'd go straight to voice mail," he replied. "Anyway. Uh...I have some bizarre news. Good, but fucking bizarre."

"Yeah?" Please tell me he'd dumped that motherfucker.

"Yeah. The Initiative received a $200,000 donation today."

"What the fuck?" I blurted out incredulously.

"Exactly. Can you believe that? When I saw the zeroes, I

was like, get the fuck outta here with that shit. There's gotta be some mistake. But no. It's legit, Nicky. Two hundred Gs."

"Madonn', I...I don't know what to say." I scrubbed a hand over my face and felt a hundred different emotions stirring within me, and among them was a creeping suspicion. Where in the fresh hell was Gideon? "Who's it from?"

"I don't know. That's what's so frustrating about it," he grated. "It was an anonymous donation."

Sure. Yeah, sure. Anonymous. I wondered if Anthony or I knew anyone with that kind of money, maybe someone who'd recently entered my life...

I huffed out a breath and looked down the street again. His driver usually drove up from that direction so he could pull up right outside the building.

"Hold up," Anthony said. "You don't think..."

"I don't know what I think." I heard the tightness in my voice and tried to calm my fucking tits. I had warning bells sounding inside my head, but it was too soon to get worked up.

Fuck. I rubbed at my chest. It felt like a giant had closed a fist around it.

The city commotion didn't sound like my favorite noise machine anymore. The sirens wailing in the distance, the honking, the occasional hollering, the steady hum of conversation from the pedestrians at the intersection twenty feet away from me, the steam billowing up from the pavement, the lights—all of it sent my heart rate up. Something was wro—

I snapped my gaze to the left as a familiar-looking Bentley rolled up, and I coulda fuckin' cried from the relief. It was him.

"I'mma have to call you back," I said, swallowing against the dryness in my throat. "Gideon just got here."

"All right, talk later."

I ended the call and caught a glance at the time. I'd nearly freaked out over his being five minutes late. If there was something wrong, it was with me. Jesus H. Christ.

"Hi." I felt like I'd just run a marathon, but seeing him calmed me down. He looked less frazzled today. He'd donned a fall coat that fit him unfairly well, as if he needed to get any sexier. And he wore that kind smile for *me*.

"I apologize for being late. There was an accident on Eighth."

I didn't care. I met him halfway and yanked him down for a hard kiss.

How fucking ironic that I'd fall in love in a New York minute.

He was caught off guard by the force at first, but then he grinned a little. "I like being greeted like this."

"Good," I chuckled. "You ready for our walk?"

He nodded. "I'd like to stop for fries somewhere, if you know a good place. I forgot to eat dinner today."

Some worry trickled in, 'cause here we go again with the forgetfulness. He was forgetting to take care of himself.

"We'll find something better," I told him, grabbing his hand. "Ya gotta eat proper food, papito."

"Fries are potatoes." He frowned. "It doesn't get much more proper than that. You're part Irish—you should know."

I barked out a laugh and hugged his bicep. "You're funny."

When was a good time to bring up the donation?

Something in Gideon's life must've changed for the better because he was a chatty Cathy today. As we strolled through a part of Hell's Kitchen, he spoke at length about Chester's latest escapades in the park and that Gideon had booked a photographer for a shoot, 'cause the dog looked "precious rolling around in the fallen leaves."

We reached the piers along the Hudson, which was usually where we started turning back toward the apartment, but now he was talking animatedly about an old goth metal band he'd found. In two days, he'd gone through their entire discography, and he couldn't stop raving about them.

That was precious.

I soaked up every word.

"...and on that note, do you ever sing?" he asked.

He'd gone from the guitar solo of a Swedish metal artist to my singing? Fair enough.

"You've heard me sing." As we passed the USS *Intrepid*, I gestured for us to cross the street while it was still green. It was time to find a place to eat.

"Not solo," he pointed out. "I've only heard you provide your brother with backup."

True. "I prefer backup and harmonies," I replied. "We have a few songs where I sing more, though. 'Stand by Me,' for instance. Which we'll be performing this Saturday." I nudged him.

"I'm looking forward to it. I'll be the stalker in the back."

I chuckled.

We walked in comfortable silence for a moment once we'd reached West 45th Street, and I thought we could take it all the way to Times Square. He'd told me he avoided the area because it was always so crowded, but then he'd also admitted that he hadn't walked below Central Park in years. Wherever he went, he got there in a car.

We made it through a residential area before he spoke up again. "I haven't felt comfortable rambling to anyone since I was young."

I kissed his shoulder, equally thrilled he had no issues being honest about those things...and bummed out, because it fucking sucked that we had no future.

He squeezed my hand. "By the way, is Nicky short for Nicholas?"

"Nicola. *No one* calls me that, not even my family, so don't get any ideas."

"Oh. But it's such a beautiful name. Don't you think I'm special enough to be granted permission to call you that?"

I laughed and peered up at his sly expression. He was trying to play me! He didn't have puppy-dog eyes, but he *was* fucking cute. And it was like he'd realized that I didn't like saying no to him.

"You're gonna have to be a lot more convincing than that," I retorted.

Damn it. The challenge lit up his eyes.

I loved that he was being playful with me. I loved it so fucking hard.

He promised he'd come up with something "shortly," and I "uh-huh"d him along as I looked up the street to see if I could spot any good restaurants.

"You don't believe me," he stated, mildly offended. "I can be quite persuasive, you know."

Don't I know it.

"I'm aware. I've been fucked by you." I missed it. "Christ. I should be the one paying you." I shook my head to myself. And while we were on the subject, I wanted to make something clear. "You know you're not a dollar sign for me, right? I mean— you were. At first. I'm saving most of the money so I can get into business with Anthony, but—"

"I know." He lifted my hand and kissed the top of it. "You've hinted at it before."

Now was the best time to bring up the donation.

"Someone donated $200,000 to the academy today," I said.

"Oh?" He schooled his features a little too quickly, and I narrowed my eyes. "That's interesting. Would you say that's a considerable donation, or...?"

What the fresh fuck.

"Considerable? It's a giant donation, and the giant question is—was it you?"

It had to be him. And I had to know why.

"Why would you assume it's me?" he asked, feigning confusion. Very poorly, I might add. He hadn't been put on this earth to become an actor. "You know what I think? I think it was someone who went to your brother's website, read the page with the vision he has for the Initiative—with music camps, tutoring, musical therapy—and the man, perhaps he has a dog, or maybe he doesn't, simply thought, that's a good cause. I'd like to support that."

I...didn't know what to say. I stopped him right then and there on the sidewalk, and I just stared at him.

He tested a barely there smile, and some uncertainty seeped into his gaze. "Please don't make a big deal out of it."

But it was a big deal. A giant deal.

I took a step closer and pressed my lips to his. I kissed him unhurriedly, wanting to say so much, but nothing came out. Not a damn word. Well, actually...there was one thing I could test the waters with.

"I don't want you to pay me another cent," I murmured. "It doesn't feel right anymore. You're...essentially paying me to be where I wanna be, right fucking here, with you."

He swallowed hard and rested his forehead to mine. "You're not terminating our arrangement, are you? I'm not ready."

I shook my head. "No, I'm just saying this has been real for me for a while, and I don't want either of us to pretend it's about the money. We're more than a transaction. So, from this minute, there's no more hiding behind a payment plan. You're with me because you wanna be with me, for however long. Deal?"

A tremor ran through him, and he cupped my face and kissed me passionately. Deeply. He swept his tongue into my mouth, he seduced me, he made out with me like it was our last kiss, he fucking owned me.

"I wasn't supposed to break any rules with you," he said raggedly against my lips. The surrender and despair in his low voice shook me. "I appreciate the gesture, and I won't hide, but the money's already yours. Tina has it—"

"I'll talk to her."

He shook his head and smiled. "Don't be stubborn. If you don't want the money, donate it. I have recommendations. There's this one place in Brooklyn called The Fender Initiative."

I huffed. "You're kind of insufferable, baby."

He rumbled a laugh and buried his face against my neck. "Forty-four years old and called baby..."

I grinned and rolled my eyes. "It's a term of endearment, dork."

"I know." He was still chuckling when he resurfaced, and it was impossible even to pretend to be annoyed. His happiness looked amazing. "Come on, I want something sweet, preferably chocolate."

"After you've eaten dinner," I reminded him.

"Chocolate for dinner sounds lovely."

"Gideon."

"Oh, fine. But no vegetables."

"And you wonder why I called you baby..."

He laughed.

Gideon was *picky*.

After he'd vetoed six different restaurants on the way to Times Square, I put my foot down and bought us hot dogs from a vendor. The horrified look he gave me was priceless. But hey, I had limits. If he had texture issues or something, fine. I wasn't gonna make him eat something he really didn't like, but the excuse "I don't know..." wasn't actually an excuse. He just couldn't make up his mind sometimes.

"Is this truly hygienic?" He eyed his hot dog with all the skepticism he could muster.

"Trust, papi." I bit into my hot dog and chewed quickly. "All eyes are on the street vendors. If you want an unsanitary dining experience, go to a midrange restaurant."

He hummed and stepped closer to the building. Times Square was right ahead, less than a minute's walk up the street, and there were plenty of benches.

"You wanna go sit over there?" I pointed up the street.

"I don't think so." He took a tentative bite of his food. He hadn't allowed anything other than mustard on it. "I know where we are. Tourist mecca of the universe."

I snickered.

He looked as if he couldn't decide if he liked the food or not, though the next bite he took was without apprehension.

I extended the water I'd bought for us in silent offering.

He shook his head, busy chewing.

I grinned when he got some mustard on his upper lip. "You're cute, you know that?"

"Don't give me compliments when I'm eating." He failed to stifle his own grin, and I could thank the bright lights from Times Square for revealing his faint blush. "I still want chocolate after this, for the record. Don't deny me."

I really fucking loved him. He'd let his guard down around me, and I never wanted it to go up again.

"There's a Godiva store across the square," I mentioned and took a big bite. Unlike his lame hot dog, I had ketchup and onions on mine too.

"Damn it." He winced as he spilled some mustard on his coat. "I like their hot chocolate very much."

"We'll get you a cup, then." I jammed the rest of my hot dog into my pie hole, then uncapped the water and poured some on a napkin. "Lemme," I said with my mouth full. Then I wiped the stain off his coat—and his upper lip. "All gone."

He smiled and dipped down to kiss me chastely. "Thank you."

I smiled back.

He didn't seem to mind that I doted on him. I ached for a lot more of it. It was one of my favorite aspects of being in a relationship, taking care of someone, making them feel special.

"If walking across Times Square will give you anxiety, you can stay here while I buy us some chocolate." I grabbed the trash and threw it in a nearby trash can. "It's one thing to push you past some discomfort, but I don't wanna expose you to panic or anything."

Gideon made a face and ran a hand through his hair. "As comfortable as it would be to say I'd panic, I don't think I would. You have a strange knack for not giving me more than I can handle." He paused. "Except for one time. When you invited your brother to come out for drinks with us, I stopped breathing for a beat."

Aw, shit. "I only asked him 'cause I knew he'd say no, hon. He's up at dawn on Saturdays. That's when he goes bananas in his workshop. He builds and repairs instruments."

"Oh. I should've known."

I shook my head and ducked in for a quick kiss. "I coulda explained it after it happened." Clear communication was important in any relationship. With someone who was autistic,

I'd learned you might as well multiply that importance by ten. "You ready to hit up Godiva?"

"Yes." He nodded firmly. "Please tell me the direction as soon as we reach the square. I'm not entirely certain I can navigate myself once I'm there."

"Of course. I'll let you know."

I noticed by his grip on my hand that he was tense and uncomfortable, but he pushed through and walked with quick strides.

"We'll have Levi's to our right here," I said as we got closer.

"You like that brand," he noted. "Most of your jeans are Levi's."

Yup.

When we reached the square, we were smack-dab in the middle of it. Billboards literally everywhere, each one flashing in bright colors and turning this little spot in New York into a constant state of daytime. It wasn't even midnight yet, so there were still tourists pretty much everywhere.

"Let's cross here," I said, pointing the water bottle at the street we'd just walked up. We needed to get to the other side. "Godiva is straight across over there." I gestured to the actual plaza where there were no cars, so we had to cross it diagonally.

Gideon nodded with a dip of his chin and followed me across the street, before he slowed down and looked up. He stared at the billboards as if he'd never seen them before. Fashion brands, Broadway shows, fast-food commercials, comedy specials, Coke, M&M, Hershey's...

It was quickly becoming too much for him, I could tell. He looked away from one flashing billboard only to get stuck on another, and then he spun around in a half circle and flinched at the sound of a street performer who was banging on upside-down buckets. I could only imagine what it was doing to Gideon, having no filters to push anything aside. People talking and laughing and hollering, taking pictures and pointing at various billboards, the traffic noise, the ever-present sound of sirens wailing. Times Square was alive.

"Gideon, we're almost there," I urged. "Focus on me—or look at the store over there."

"I—" He flinched again and came to a full stop. "It's too much."

"I know, hon. Let me guide you to the benches, okay? Just a few seconds."

He sucked in a breath and nodded once.

I had to think fast. He was gonna panic if he didn't get away from all the noise and the movement, but it was a struggle to make him budge at all. The nearest bench was ten or so feet away, and I had to almost shove him there.

Fuck, what would Anthony do? He'd dealt with students' meltdowns.

How could I create a safe bubble or whatever?

I could only think of one thing.

"Here, sit down. One leg on each side." I managed to get him to sit down on the stone bench, and then I hiked one of his legs over it before I straddled the bench myself.

"This isn't n-normal," he gritted out and screwed his eyes shut. "*Fuck.*"

First time I heard Gideon swear, and it was because I'd pushed him too far. Fucking great.

"Adults don't sit like this, N-Nicky," he insisted.

"Fuck being an adult, then." I scooted closer and hitched my legs over his thighs. The water bottle ended up slightly behind me. At the same time, I dug out my earbuds and my phone from my jacket pocket. "Let's shut out the world, shall we?"

He let me insert one of the buds.

I took the remaining bud and picked my latest playlist.

Conveniently one with love songs that I'd selected because of the man in front of me.

A slower pop song about new love in New York started playing, and I popped the collar of his coat to provide somewhat of a barrier.

"It's just us here." I pressed our foreheads together and dropped my phone between us. "We're the only ones who matter right now. Just us. And the song."

His rapid breaths misted in the air, and I did what I could to encourage slower breathing. I snuck one hand inside his coat and placed it on his hip where he could feel my fingers tap out the beat of the song, in hopes his breathing would match it. Wait, fuck, was the beat too fast? It was too fast. Christ, I was an idiot.

I hurriedly picked up my phone and scrolled—perfect. One of the latest-played songs was not only slower, but it had something Gideon had asked for.

I pushed play on the recording of Anthony and me playing "Cages," a song in which I sang almost as much as he did. My brother on the piano, me on the guitar, singing about failed expectations, searching in the darkness, and fighting uphill battles.

The song flooded my senses, and I slid my hand up his chest instead, making sure I didn't press too hard. I tapped the slow beat over his pounding heart and gently nudged him to rest his forehead on my shoulder instead. I'd close my jacket around him if I could.

"That's you," he rasped. "It's your voice."

I nodded and kissed him behind his ear. "Try to breathe with the beat."

He shuddered.

Halfway through the song, I thought I could detect the slightest improvement, so I put the song on repeat for now.

I kept my cheek pressed to his ear, reckoning it blocked out some of the outside noise, and rubbed his neck absently.

"Your voice is soothing," he muttered. "Anthony's is more...tortured."

Fitting word.

"I'm quite partial to y-yours, but I might be biased."

I smiled against his skin. "Bias is underrated."

He choked a little laugh that almost sounded like a whimper, and it slashed worry through me. I inched back enough to be able to see his face. Motherfucker. A tear was rolling down his cheek, and I wiped it away with my thumb.

I hugged him to me and cursed myself to the fiery pits of hell. Why the hell had I brought him here?

"I shouldn't have pushed you to do this, Gideon. I'm so fucking sorry. It won't happen again."

"Stop it." He gathered my hands against his chest, and I felt that his heart had slowed down significantly. "Anxiety and panic won't kill me, Nicky. I'll take a panic attack every day of the week if I don't have to go through it alone. You're the f-first one who..." He sucked in a breath and trailed off.

As much as I itched to hear the rest of that sentence, he needed to cool it. He was just calming down. Talking could wait.

"Focus on breathing," I murmured. "Do you want some water?"

He shook his head. "I want to go back to your place. And I want chocolate."

I chuckled silently. He was coming back to me. "Okay. Here's what we're gonna do. You put both earbuds in, and we'll pick some metal you like. Then I'll guide you over to Godiva."

"All right."

When he lifted his head, I twisted my body and pointed

across the street, closer to the eastern corner of the plaza. "See the Godiva sign over there?"

He followed my gaze and nodded.

"Okay. I'll lead the way. You just focus on the music and following me."

"I will. But I saw something in your playlist I'd like to hear. I'm curious about what you enjoy."

I handed him my phone and watched him scroll through the playlist I'd originally played, the one with love songs, and he picked one called "Slow Dance."

It took him thirty-eight seconds to quirk a brow at me. "A hip-hop song that's anything but slow...about slow dancing?"

I laughed. "This ain't hip-hop." I'd call it mainstream pop with some R&B elements. "I like the beat." I bobbed my head and swayed a little.

He mustered a faint smile. Then he glanced up at the Coca-Cola billboard behind me that Times Square would be nothing without, and he appeared more content now.

"It's a spectacular place when I don't have to listen to it," he admitted.

"The sounds are worse than the billboards?"

"Much." He nodded. "City noise is unpredictable when it's too close. I like having it in the background at home and so on, but being a pedestrian in this city is a headache."

"But you like our walks...?"

"I love them," he corrected. "I just make sure to prepare myself beforehand."

Made sense.

We'd had a little too much of the unpredictable tonight, though, so I wanted to get him home as soon as possible.

"Come on. Chocolate, then home." I untangled myself from him and left the bench, losing my earbud in the process.

He took it and inserted it in his other ear.

CHAPTER 9

"Honey...your alarm..."

"Is a menace," he grumbled sleepily.

Once he'd turned it off, he returned to me and pressed our bodies together, one hand sliding down my back to squeeze my ass cheeks. Then he released a long sigh and stretched out alongside me.

"I don't want to work today," he yawned. "I want to stay right here all day and cuddle and eat fries and feel ridiculously cherished whenever you call me baby or papi or honey. But my newest favorite is papito. You only use it when you take care of me."

"That's when you're my little Daddy." I chuckled drowsily and buried my face against his neck.

What was less funny was his lack of mentioning sex. We'd gone almost five days now without him fucking me. I'd hinted at it here and there. I'd asked if he was curious about bottoming, to which he'd made a face and shaken his head. I didn't care. I was a bottom through and through, but I'd thought by suggesting new things, he might...wake up. It wasn't as if he wasn't still sexual with me. He rendered me breathless and stupid every damn night with blow jobs and massages and whatnot. Just... nothing for himself. He was "tired."

"Come here." He turned onto his side and dipped down, capturing my mouth with his. "Friday is the worst day of them all."

Because it was my day "off."

"Mm..." I inched back and wet my bottom lip. "How can you still taste like chocolate?"

I'd bought him a fairly big box of chocolate at Godiva earlier this week, along with a large cup of hot chocolate, and he'd snatched a few pieces here and there whenever he was with me. But after a long night of sleeping, not to mention we'd brushed our teeth together like some sappy, love-sick couple yesterday, it didn't make sense.

"It's possible I grabbed the last two pieces when I got up to use the bathroom an hour ago," he confessed.

I grinned lazily and kissed him again. "Christ, I—" *love you.* "Can't get over how fucking cute you are sometimes."

There was no going back for me. After our adventure to Times Square, we'd come back here, and I'd asked him to finish the sentence he hadn't been able to complete earlier. He'd admitted that I was the first one, aside from his parents, who made him feel like he didn't have to worry about composure and always being on top of things. And it'd just sealed my fate. I was gonna be one miserable fuck for an eternity when this was over.

"Want me to whip up some breakfast before you go?" I asked.

I wasn't surprised when he declined. He'd only let me do it once, then abruptly declared he couldn't afford to get hooked on my spoiling him. Only, he'd used fancier words.

"What're you going to do today?" He rolled out of bed with a grunt and reached for his discarded clothes on my chair at the keyboard. "Practice with the choir, I assume?"

"Not until tomorrow morning," I replied. "Today I got brunch with Tina, then work. We have a recital at the academy." It was that time of year. There would be a recital every Friday until the semester was over.

Gideon glanced back at me as he zipped up his pants. "You can't return the money when you see Tina. You gave me your word."

"I *won't*." I stretched out and groaned, hoping I'd get another couple hours of sleep soon.

After putting on his undershirt, Gideon began buttoning his regular shirt. It fit him to a fucking tee. "What kind of recital is it?"

I smiled instinctively, beyond proud of my students. "So, every year, Anthony and I put up lists in the hallway at the first entrance where kids can decide what project they wanna be part of at the end of their semester. Today is my soft rock performance for those who've played their instruments three years or longer." Which meant it was a group of seventeen hormonal teenagers, mostly between the ages of thirteen and fifteen, except for two eleven-year-old prodigies. Among them was David; he and I would share a piano tonight and sing together. He was only on his second year of playing the piano, but he was fucking brilliant already.

Before I knew it, I sat up in bed and rambled to Gideon as he continued getting dressed.

"Three students from Anthony's saxophone class are joining us too," I said. "And three boys and three girls from the freshman choir. They're fucking adorable. You should hear them. Their voices—" I kissed my fingertips.

Gideon grinned tiredly and threw his tie around his neck. "My voice at fourteen was anything but adorable."

"Right?" I chuckled. "We have one guy who's worried about his voice cracking, so he's staying away from anything high-pitched."

How could he make tying a tie look so pornographic?

"Sounds like a good time," he responded. "I take it your auditorium will be filled to the max with proud parents."

Sort of. Our auditorium was tiny; it was one of the reasons we split the end-of-semester recitals into smaller groups, because there were only seats for seventy-five people.

"There's room for one more if you...you know...have nothing better to do."

I saw the eager agreement in his eyes before he accepted the invitation verbally, and it made my day. Not only would I see him tonight too, but his genuine interest in my work meant the world to me.

Then I pointed out jokingly that it wasn't fair that he came to see me in Brooklyn while I knew virtually nothing about his personal life.

"What's there to share?" He crawled onto the bed and leaned over for a kiss. "I don't come from a family that hosts Sunday dinners or organizes outdoor concerts with their local church. I see my cousins and their extended families for major holidays—the ones I don't see at work every day." He got my lips again before he straightened up. "I have an elderly neighbor who comes over sometimes to pet Chester and recommend a new wine she's tried, and I have one friend from college with whom I meet up for dinner perhaps twice a year—unless he has to cancel because he has three daughters all active in various sports." He blew out a breath, grabbing his suit jacket, and he faced me. "Under normal circumstances, I'd be with Claire for dinner most evenings, but I haven't seen her since our arrangement began. My social life isn't anything to write home about, so to speak."

I pinched my lips together and processed everything, and I didn't have much to say in response, other than that I wanted to replace a few people in his life with some cool people from this little place called Brooklyn.

"What time is the recital tonight?" he asked.

"Seven," I replied. "First entrance—not the one you used last time. Just follow the herd."

"I'll be there."

———

Fifteen minutes to showtime and I was stuck to a six-year-old girl whose mother had just called in tears to apologize and say she was gonna be late picking up her daughter. Li'l Maya was a happy sprite who'd joined our kiddie choir this semester as part of her therapy to lose her stutter.

Now she didn't wanna let go of my hand.

"Five minutes till the doors open, guys!" I hollered. "I want everyone on stage within a minute!"

"And phones off!" Anthony reminded as he appeared with two more chairs. Presumably for the guitarist and bass player. "You want them here?"

I nodded. It looked good. Drums, bass, guitars, and tambourines to the front right, sax players and choir standing in the back, then David and me on the piano to the front left.

We had two younger instructors helping out in the back, and they could deal with the girls' panicking about makeup and wardrobe. This was about the music; there was no creative theme or papier-mâché scenery to speak of. We'd put up blue velvet curtains and a blue velvet background, and everyone had on a black "TGI Fender" tee. That was enough.

The sax players and a few others walked past Maya and me to do a quick sound check, and David followed shortly after. It was my cue to free up my hands, so I squatted down to Maya's level.

"You sure you don't wanna wait with Angela, hon?" I asked, referring to one of our instructors. "She has grapes and juice boxes..."

Maya shook her head stubbornly and tightened her grip on my hand. "I'mma wait w-wiv you."

I threw a helpless look toward Anthony, who was watching the exchange, and his own expression left it up to me. *What do you wanna do?* I didn't fucking know, but we were out of time, so I had to improvise.

We couldn't have her getting upset backstage.

"One minute till the doors open!" Anthony called to everyone.

The last two stragglers from the choir darted onto the stage, and my brother closed the curtains.

"Fuck it," I muttered and picked up Maya. "Try not to steal the show, brown eyes." I touched one of her bouncy curls and earned myself a toothless grin. "No grabbing the microphone, no touching the keys on the piano. Gabeesh?"

"G'bish!" She nodded. "Can I w-wave?"

I laughed and joined David on the bench, and I situated her sideways across my lap. "You can wave when all the people have sat down, and then when we start playing, you keep your little paws to yourself. How's that?"

She nodded seriously. "I keep 'em here." She folded her arms over her chest and tucked her hands close to her body.

"That's perfect," I chuckled. Turning to David, I offered a reassuring smile at his raised brows that he aimed at Maya, before I turned back to the rest of the ensemble. "Everyone ready? Anthony's about to open the doors."

The kids responded with nervous nods and murmurs of "sure" and "ready."

"Remember to have fun," I urged. "I don't wanna be the only one with ants in my pants."

From the older teenagers, that earned me a couple eye-rolls. It seemed they had to be indifferent now, but they'd had no issues clownin' off at rehearsal earlier. The sax players had even come up with a dance. I hoped they felt brave enough to have at it.

Maya grabbed the pocket of my jeans and peered inside. "You got an-n-nts?"

I smiled widely and shook my head. "Just an expression. There are no ants, I promise."

"Phew." She grinned goofily.

Seconds later, the auditorium filled with the sounds of parents, siblings, and grandparents. There was always a pang in my chest because I knew not all the kids had someone in the audience. It was why Anthony and I made sure to record each recital, so the students could show their folks at home. I knew Carmen, in particular, was bummed out about her dad not being able to make it. He couldn't get off work. But he'd see her fantastic progress with her saxophone online.

As my brother gave us a brief introduction on the other side of the curtain, telling the family members a little about what we'd worked on this semester, David stretched his fingers and rolled his shoulders like he'd watched me do so many times.

My little wonder boy. Kid could go far if he kept this up.

When Anthony was done, I made eye contact with everyone one last time and nodded, 'cause this was it. It was time to show their nonnas how it was done.

The curtains were rolled back to the sound of parents applauding, and Maya waved merrily to everyone the second the spotlights hit us. I stifled my chuckle and adjusted the mic between David and me, and there was no other intro. I counted us down from four, my stomach fluttered, I wondered where Gideon was sitting—or if he was one of those standing in the back—and about a hundred tiny other thoughts flitted past in my mind right before my fingers hit the piano keys.

"Lonely with Me" by Parachute was a good upbeat song to start things off with, and if Gideon happened to read into the choice of song, I'd consider it a bonus.

David joined in a couple lines later, as did the drums, bass, and guitars.

Baby...

I'll be wherever you are.

The most explosive entrance belonged to the choir and the sax players who filled in during the chorus, and it was im-fuck-ing-possible to withhold my grin as I sang. They were so goddamn good. My chest swelled with pride, and Maya forgot my instructions and clapped excitedly.

I was ready to join my brother here full time. This was my dream. We were gonna expand. His vision was mine too.

Baby...

You shouldn't be lonely.

Before this recital was over, we were gonna get a damn standing ovation, 'cause we were killing it. The energy flowing through us was something else. All the nerves had taken a hike, and the students were moving to the beat we created together.

The same energy buzzed through us the following evening when Anthony and I found ourselves standing on a stage in a run-down, abandoned church at the edge of Williamsburg. Heaters along the brick walls and bistro lights in the broken ceiling threw a warm glow over the packed church for the fifth year in a row.

One big spotlight was trained on the stage and showing how much we could sweat.

We were on our last session for the evening, and the families with young children had gone home. It allowed us to raise the nonexistent roof of this place, and we weren't the only ones. Out of the approximately two hundred Solo cups in the crowd, I estimated half of them had more bourbon than hot cider.

I bobbed my head and plucked at the strings of my precious Gibson guitar, flirting with Anthony's flawless playing on the piano, though the gospel choir behind us owned all of us. They were the ones who fueled us, the ones who made the atmosphere around us fucking crackle.

Music filled my soul.

Gideon filled my heart.

He'd shown up late because Chester had eaten something he shouldn't and had thrown up all over Gideon's home. The dog was feeling better now, but I had a feeling Gideon would go home fairly quickly after the show was over. Not that his worry had stopped him from buying four—that's right, four—hot dogs from a vendor, as well as two cups of hot chocolate and a deep-fried Snickers.

I was pretty sure I'd seen him buy raffle tickets too.

Anthony and I exchanged a quick look as the song drew to its close, and we stopped playing at the same time, leaving the last few seconds for the choir and Luiz on the drums.

Fuck me, I was spent. I wiped my forehead with the sleeve of my shirt as the crowd applauded.

Last song. It'd been a hectic week, and it felt like the last two months had led up to this moment.

Nerves tightened my stomach, and I swallowed dryly.

Anthony let out a whistle, causing me to glance over at him, and he nodded at...something.

I followed his gaze over the crowd, instinctively seeking out Gideon near the western wall where he'd been standing before —and fuck me so hard and then kill me. *Mamma mia*, why? Just why? Why was Pop talking to him? Of all the visitors, not to mention some of Pop's actual *friends*, he had to wander over to a complete stranger with whom I happened to wanna spend the rest of my life?

My father wasn't generally an observant man. Had it been Nonna... Let's just say there'd been a reason I hadn't sought out Gideon in the crowd when she was still here, 'cause she could sniff out a story from a mile away.

"We have one more song for y'all," Anthony said into the mic. "Couple weeks ago, Nicky came to me and said we had to play this one, and he wouldn't really tell me why."

What the fuck, dude?

I scowled back at him.

He smiled, perfectly at ease, and went on. "We've performed it together before, so I said shoot. It was nice to have a tune we didn't have to rehearse, considering how little time we had." He paused. "Yesterday we had a recital over at the Initiative, and Nicky sang with his group of students. Now listen, I've always told the little shit he should sing more than he does." He got several laughs from that. I wasn't on the same page. At fucking all. What was he playing at? "But something different last night," he said. "His voice was stronger. And I happen to know...because it's what our nonna always says... We sing better when we have someone to sing for." That motherfucker. Without another word, he sang the first line from "Stand by Me," and I acted on autopilot.

My fingers fell over the strings, and I had no choice but to walk over to my own microphone and face the crowd.

Because for some idiotic reason, I'd asked to turn this into a duet rather than be his backup.

I joined in on the first chorus and closed my eyes. It was just better. I knew Gideon was watching and listening. That was enough. The rest of the world could fuck off, and so could my nervousness, if I was gonna be honest. *Cazzo.*

Thankfully, it worked. The music swept me away, and even I thought I sang better than usual. More than that, my guitar became an extension of me. We built up a crescendo, and the choir pushed us toward an edge—where Anthony and I just stopped. I drew an unsteady breath that sounded too loud, and then Luiz set us on fire with the drums. Anthony and I raised the tempo and the volume, backed off and quieted down, went up toward the edge again, then back down.

In a quiet moment, I smiled to myself and pictured Gideon's face before me. It was *the* song to impress him. The very one. I plucked at the strings and improvised a technical lick, then slid my fingers along the strings and made the music wail for me in a bluesy, full-blown solo. As if my guitar had its own tortured voice.

Anthony followed, Luiz followed, the choir followed. We built up everything once more until we all jumped off the ledge and belted out the last chorus till our lungs burned for air.

Stand by me, darlin'.

Choose me.

Pick me, god-fucking-dammit.

CHAPTER 10

I was stalling.

The gig had left me a little too raw, and I had to at least compose myself somewhat before I faced Gideon. So I took my time helping Anthony box up our instruments and equipment.

Pop gave no fucks and stepped up on the platform, hands in his pockets, his ugly old bucket hat on as always, and an open jacket to show his The Fender Initiative sweater. Our old man was as unpolished and politically incorrect as they came, but he had a heart of gold and had always supported us in his own clumsy way.

"Youse rocked it tonight, eh?" He bobbed his head in agreement with his own statement. "No one was sitting at the end. I saw." He gestured at the floor. It was starting to clear out. As always, too many were dumping their lawn chairs and "forgetting" their blankets. Same shit every year. "Everyone cheering—that's good."

"Thanks, Pop." I bundled together the cord to my amplifier and walked over to kiss his cheek. "Anthony drivin' you home?"

"Yeah, since Nonna took my car," he replied.

"Don't catch a cold, old man," Anthony hollered from over by the drums. He was helping Luiz pack up. "Go have some coffee under a heater."

Pop snorted and jerked his thumb at Anthony while he eyed me. "When did that boy become my father, huh? That's what I wanna know."

I grinned and started taking apart the microphone stand.

Then he wagged a finger at me. "And you. Either you're stupid, or you think I'm stupid. You can't sing like a canary to Ruby and Camila and don't expect shit to get back to your grandmother and me. Huh? The fuck's wrong witchu?"

I winced. "What've they told you?"

"All about that suit in the back." He jerked his chin, presumably at Gideon. "You've been shacking up with him in the city."

I shoulda known about Ruby. Her grandmother talked to Nonna, who talked to everyone, including Ruby herself, and she wasn't the best at resisting my grandmother's ways. But there were limits, and I knew I could count on my friend not to spill the beans about how Gideon and I met.

"So that's why you were giving him the third degree," I said.

"Third degree," he scoffed. "I was just making sure you wasn't bringing home a mamaluke like that one did." He nodded at Anthony.

I was too nervous to laugh, but I probably would later.

"Anyway." Pop twirled a finger and got serious. "Bring the boy over for dinner once he's stopped calling youse 'just friends.'" Ouch. But I hadn't expected Gideon to call us anything else. "He seems nice—maybe a little uptight, but you can't be picky anymore, son. You ain't twenty no more, and you wanna find a good man before your balls start sagging."

"For chrissakes!" I hollered.

"What?!" He widened his arms. "I'm just sayin'!"

"Can I turn thirty first?!"

"Ay, both'a yas!" Anthony called.

I growled under my breath and tried to reel it in. My temper, not my pre-sagging balls.

"I give you two love and good advice," Pop argued, speaking with his hands, "and what do I get in return? You stomp on my heart."

"Oh, for—you've been spending too much time at Nonna's," I told him irritably. "How about you take care of your own sagging balls? Go meet a nice lady who didn't change your diapers as a baby!"

"Why the fuck would I do that for?" He frowned. "If I sell the cow, the neighborhood women won't bring me casseroles when I dangle the milk in front of them."

I groaned and scrubbed my hands over my face. "I give up."

"Might as well. And go talk to the boy!" he ordered.

Madonn', if Gideon thought it was funny when I called him baby, it had nothing on when Pop called him *boy*.

"I will, 'cause you're givin' me a headache." I jabbed a finger at my temple and dumped the last cords in a hardcase box. "All the fuckin' drama all the fuckin' time."

"Easy," he bitched. "This is still a house of God. Don't curse."

I shot him an incredulous look.

He grinned and scratched his nose. "What?"

I just shook my head and walked off the stage.

Gideon was standing some twenty feet away, close enough to have probably heard most of that exchange, and the closer I got, the more I thought he looked troubled. His worry wrinkles were in full effect in his forehead.

He was holding a glazed bear claw in one hand and a bunch of napkins in the other.

"Hey, you." I came to a stop before him and told myself to keep my cool. For all I knew, he was still worried about his dog.

He waved his pastry at the stage. "No one even reacted when you fought with your father."

I frowned, confused. "Fought? That wasn't a fight."

"It looked like a fight. It sounded like a fight."

Aw, fuck. I rubbed the back of my neck and glanced at Pop and Anthony over my shoulder. They were shooting the shit and stacking boxes together.

"That's just how we talk sometimes, hon. We can be pretty loud, I guess." I turned back to Gideon again. "We're good, but I'm sorry I didn't get the chance to warn you about Pop. I under-estimated the power of rumors, and now they think we're dating."

"Oh." He dropped his stare to the ground, or the pastry in his hand, and nodded slowly. "I apologize. You were... I can't find the words. The way you performed tonight—I felt it every-where. It was overwhelmingly beautiful."

"But something's wrong." I took a step forward and tried to make eye contact, and if I didn't find out what was up with him soon, I'd flip my fucking shit. "Talk to me, Gideon."

He winced and clutched his side. "I am incredibly nause-ated. I had six hot dogs. Can you take this?"

Mother of—!

I quickly accepted the bear claw, then ushered him toward two abandoned lawn chairs near a wall. "Why would you eat that much? Now you're gonna have a stomachache. I swear—you make me worry, papito."

"It wasn't my fault," he argued weakly. "I'm a nervous eater sometimes. Specifically when I don't know protocol and there are no known social cues to pick up on. I-I didn't know what to say to your father, and then there was the lady selling the hot dogs. She looked so happy when I bought the food. She was raving about the charities some of the proceeds go to."

Christ. My sweet man. I shouldn't have unleashed him on his own, smack-dab in the middle of a Catholic community. We had our ways of making people open their wallets.

I helped him sit down before I took my seat next to him.

"There are two socially accepted activities to occupy your hands with when you arrive alone at a social event," he informed me. "You can stare at your phone, or you can eat and drink. Checking my phone seems rude in my world, so..." So, he'd eaten. A lot.

"What's the story about this one?" I held up the bear claw.

He eyed it wistfully. "It looked tasty. I might want it in a moment."

I shook my head and set down the pastry on the ground. "Nonna makes the best bear claws—with even more glaze. When you feel better, I'll get you a bunch. Okay? I think you need to rest your stomach for the night."

"Perhaps you're right." He could not look more sullen.

I rubbed his back, trying not to let my amusement show, and hoped it would be safe to run and grab my jacket soon. There were no other family members he could run into—or friends, for that matter. And it was freaking brick here. I couldn't stop shuddering from the cold.

"So what turned you into a nervous eater tonight?" I wondered. "You were inhaling hot dogs before my pop came over to you."

He sighed and stared at his lap. "I have a lot on my mind. Then Chester today... I'm worried about him." He checked his watch and cringed. "I was hoping to convince you to spend more time with me, but I should head home and check in on him."

I had a feeling I knew the gist of the things he had on his mind.

It was mildly terrifying to acknowledge that he held my happiness and the future I wanted in his hands, especially since I knew without an ounce of doubt that he was going to choose his fiancée. Not for her sake, probably, but for the chance to have a family, to have children, to ensure a lifetime of stability.

I was confident enough in us to believe that he would've chosen me if he didn't dream about all those other things.

My family was amazing in my eyes; it was full of warmth and banter and affectionate madness, but we would never be called structured or...heh, stable.

"I think I'll stay here tonight." I looked over at Anthony. Maybe I could drag him out for a copious amount of booze tonight. I didn't wanna be alone in my temporary apartment in the city. I was sick of temporary.

"You can't sleep in a church that looks like Germany before it was restored after the war," Gideon argued, bewildered.

I smiled and patted his leg. "I meant with my brother."

His shoulders sagged. "Oh. Good." He peered skyward. "I genuinely don't understand how you're even allowed to host events here."

I looked up too. Much of the ceiling was gone, and there were major holes in the walls. The church was literally in ruins. All the pews long gone.

"They removed all the glass and made sure nothing was loose," I said. "But I'm sure there's a little 'I know a guy who knows a guy' involved."

"And what, a permit fell off a truck?" he asked skeptically.

I laughed. "Maybe? I don't know. I'm not in charge. But a brick hasn't moved in the five years we've held this show here."

"Hmpf." He wasn't satisfied but dropped the topic and grabbed my hand. "I will still see you tomorrow night, right?"

"Of course." I squeezed his hand.

I'd cling for as long as I could, 'cause it was all I had.

Anthony and I were dead on our feet once we'd dropped off the equipment at the academy and made it back to his place. All the good bars in his area closed within the hour, so we decided to bundle up and bring a couple six-packs up to the roof.

There were three condos in his brownstone, and Anthony's place was on the third floor, with the rooftop terrace belonging to only him. That was the kind of gold you could strike when you'd dated someone who'd bought the condo before Park Slope was gentrified. Anthony had bought it from his first love for a fraction of what it was worth after an amicable breakup because the ex, who'd been significantly older, had landed a job in Arizona where he'd been from.

That guy had to be nearing seventy now. I remembered he'd been like thirty years older than Anthony.

"I've been thinking," I said.

"So have I, but you can go first." He fiddled with the heater above the wicker sofa.

I didn't care about the dead leaves and dirt; I just sat my ass down on the creaky sofa and twisted the cap off a beer. The terrace was small, just big enough for a cramped seating area, but it hadn't stopped Anthony from buying potted trees that sat along the waist-high wall—along with pots of herbs on the edge. All dead. He sucked at keeping them alive, and the lemon tree was never gonna bear any fruit. But bless him for trying, I guess.

"No bullshit," I told him. "I wanna know what you see in

Shawn. Genuinely. He's the opposite of your type. Lay it on me."

"Seriously? This again?" He flicked on the heater once it was plugged in and sat down next to me.

Our feet landed on the low table in front of us, and I just waited for him to get to it.

Because yeah, *seriously*.

"I'm just sayin'," I said. "You used to shop for men in the geriatric ward."

He snorted. "Old isn't actually my type, jackass. I just prefer maturity."

"Oh! Oh, so *that's* why you bagged and tagged Shawn, the diva of his kindergarten, because he's *mature*."

I rolled my eyes.

Anthony didn't have the fight in him. He blew out a breath that misted in the air. "He's safe, Nicky. That's what it boils down to. You and Pop get on my ass about how he takes advantage, but that's the thing. He's not capable of taking anything of value from me. I don't give him money anymore, for the record."

I side-eyed him and took a swig of my beer.

"We *are* approaching our expiration date," he added, "but I'mma let this run its course until he gets bored. He wants constant attention, and I'm tired of it. It isn't worth the company."

It was his choice, but it didn't feel right. Anthony had so much to give. Being with someone just for the company and sticking to "safe..." Fuck, I hated it. Fuck safe.

"So, you don't even love him," I said.

He shrugged a little and leaned his head back against the wall. "Whatever it was is pretty much gone." He lolled his head my way and said, "My turn. Why the fuck are you and Gideon still pretending to have some business arrangement? You've clearly lost your shit over the man, and he doesn't seem to be any different. He's come to see you here four times. Church rehearsal, choir rehearsal, student recital, and then tonight. I don't think Shawn's come to see me that many times in the entire time we've dated."

"I—"

"And the donation? Come on."

I huffed in frustration and ran a hand through my hair. "I don't know what to say. You're kinda preaching to the choir, 'cause I want more. He's the one who's engaged to a woman who can give him kids."

"How is that a valid reason in today's day and age?" he laughed, confused. "There's adoption, there's surrogacy. Most of my gay friends today have kids."

I knew that. It was hard to explain. "I think it's a bigger-picture thing. His way of clinging to structure is to go the traditional route."

"Structure," he repeated. "Hmm."

Yeah. Structure.

I shivered as an icy wind blew past.

The heater could work better.

"What kind of structure do you have in your relationship?" he asked, patting his pockets. He retrieved his smokes and lighter. "And spare me the details."

I chuckled.

I had to think back a little. Gideon and I had established a handful of routines during our short relationship, and they had evolved into something different over time. Usually when he grew bolder and opened up more.

"He's been consistently dominant in the bedroom," I answered. It was the easiest one to start with. "I kinda wanna believe that I'm more dominant the rest of the time, though. I love taking care of him and making sure he eats and sleeps properly. He's my papito."

Anthony hummed and lit up a smoke. "I'm not surprised. You're a natural caregiver."

"And he needs it, I think," I said. "It isn't a matter of what he's capable of—the man has taken care of himself all this life. It's just...with me, the leash isn't as short."

"What do you mean?"

"Like how he's closed himself in," I answered. "He created this box—to use his words—where everything was safe and running on a perfect schedule. He didn't give himself any room to push boundaries and try new things."

"Okay, I'm with you." Anthony nodded. "You're more like a doting mother, but you're not afraid to shove the fears outta someone."

"I'm not like a mother." I slapped his arm.

He chuckled. "You fucking are, bambino. I know because I'm the same. I saw you fuss over him tonight. It's cute."

Fine, he had me there.

"That's why I think you should put yourself out there," he told me. "Tell him you want more. Fight for him. Lead the way like you've led the way so far. Maybe he needs it." He tapped his temple. "Think about it. If he's unsure, he could get stuck. Breaking patterns is hard on most of us, and we don't gotta worry about anxiety."

He had a point.

I chewed on the inside of my cheek.

"Tell him what a life with you could be like," he finished.

What *could* a life with me be like?

"I gotta say, he brings out the best in you, little brother."

I had to agree. Gideon centered me too. He calmed me down a little, and I liked it.

"Tonight, you were..." Anthony let out a whistle. "You reached a new level. Same with the recital."

I smirked and drained my first beer. Yeah, tonight had been good.

"I can't wait for Nashville," I said. "It'll be mad."

"Mm." He nodded slowly and took a swig. "I'll be heading down a week before the festival, by the way."

"Huh?" I looked to him, puzzled. We were gonna charter a bus and go all of us together.

For some reason, Anthony appeared uncomfortable. Not in a serious way, more like he was embarrassed by something.

"Don't give me shit," he warned me. "There's a food festival I wanna go to, and I haven't taken a vacation in years."

I furrowed my brow. "Why would I give you shit for that?"

Hell, I was all for him taking some time off.

He cleared his throat. "I remember last time I took a cooking class..."

I started snickering. I couldn't fucking help it. Leave it to my brother to fail at boiling spaghetti. He was a lousy Italian.

"Yeah, that's what I'm talking about," he grated. "Fuck you."

I cracked up and reached for another beer.

Man, I needed that laugh.

"Okay, what, so there're cooking classes at this festival?" I chuckled.

He nodded curtly. "I won a ticket from this chef I follow on Instagram."

Sweet baby Jesus, I was so fucking torn. Part of me wanted to laugh my ass off, but the bigger part of me just found him adorable. It was Anthony in a nutshell. He followed old students on Insta to give them praise and encouragement, and I could picture him fawning over some chef too. In his own way. He wasn't exactly fanboy material—he was too rough around the edges for that—but if he liked someone, in any way, he wanted to let them know. He always showed appreciation. It was sweet as hell.

I suppressed my amusement and tried to be less of a dick. "How did you win it?"

He shrugged, acting indifferent and bitchy. "There was a giveaway. He asked his followers to write in a comment the last thing we'd made for dinner. So I wrote 'Oatmeal, because it's the one thing I can't mess up.'"

Le-fucking-git. Coincidentally, the times he'd tried to make pasta, it ended up looking like oatmeal.

"Here." He trapped his beer between his knees and pulled out his phone. A few clicks later, and he was showing me the profile of this chef. "That's him."

And *he* had a Pride flag emoji in his bio; were we not gonna mention that?

"My hope is to leave Nashville with the ability to cook at least one good dinner," he said.

"Hon, are you sure that's your only hope?" I grabbed the phone and squinted at the profile photo. That Southern gentleman was easy on the eyes, so to speak. Charming smile, fair bit of gray in his hair, dimples, flannel, arms folded over his chest, and solid forearm game.

"Quit it." Anthony ripped the phone from me and pocketed it. "He's happily married to another chef. I follow him too. He's funny. Drops more curses than ingredients in his tutorials."

I chuckled. "Fair enough. I'm glad you're going, though. You need a vacation. And if you happen to learn how to cook pasta... that's just an awesome bonus."

He let out a laugh and finished his beer.

I chugged a little too.

Since we were already on the Nashville topic, I mentioned our set list and that we had to sit down soon and hammer out the details. Marco, our regular bass player, had already backed out, so we'd asked Chris to join us, and he was all for it. He needed a break from work too. And frankly, I was relieved. Marco was great for smaller gigs and especially if the church was involved, but we were hoping to push for more rock n' roll at this festival, and that was where Chris was better.

Anthony told me that he'd go through our recordings too. That way, we'd be able to sell a demo or two at the event, along with some merch. By using a few songs we'd already recorded, we wouldn't have to waste a bunch of dough recording new material. It would be a while before our new studio at the academy was ready, so we'd like to rent as little studio time elsewhere as possible.

Then my brother insisted on steering the conversation back to Gideon by suggesting that maybe he'd come with us to Nashville.

"That's a big maybe," I muttered against the bottle. Fuck, empty. Peering at the six-pack I'd brought, I wondered how there were only two bottles left. Three left in Anthony's.

"You'll get your answer tomorrow," he replied firmly. "In fact, I'll drive you up there myself."

I threw him a frown and reached for one more beer.

"Ruby and I already talked about it." He shrugged.

"Ay, get your own model queen best friend—Ruby's mine."

He rolled his eyes.

"I'm serious. Why're youse talking?"

"We made a pact years ago," he said with a dismissive wave. "If either of us think you're struggling with something, we talk behind your back to come up with a strategy to get you outta your funk."

"Wow." I stared at him, and I tried to wrap my brain around what he'd said, but the beers had slowed down the machinery. "Just wow, Anthony."

He laughed.

I shook my head. "Tomorrow, I'm texting all your buddies. I want a pact too."

He found that hilarious for some reason.

"So, what exactly did you agree on?" I asked.

Another chuckle slipped out before he sighed contentedly and reached for his smokes. "That I'll drive you to Gideon's, and she'll be on standby with backup plans in case you get bad news and need to get hammered."

Ouch. Well, at least they were being realistic about it.

"We don't want you to throw yourself into the nearest night-club to forget your troubles, bambino," he explained more soberly. "That's all. Judging by what you've told us—and what I've seen of this man—you two have something worth building on."

I knew we did. Even Gideon knew it. The question was whether or not it trumped the original alternative.

A rock the size of Mount Everest tumbled down into my stomach, and I blew out a breath and set the beer on the table. I didn't wanna drink no more.

"Hey." He nudged me with his elbow. "That face won't sell shit tomorrow, Nicky. You can only fight for him if you believe it's worth it."

He was right, but he was kinda ruining the beginning of my pity party.

"I can't feel a little sorry for myself?" I asked.

He smiled and shook his head. "Nope. But we can change the subject if you want. Next week, I want to sit down and make us official partners in the Initiative. Fifty-fifty on everything."

He knew just how to derail my thoughts and brighten my mood.

CHAPTER 11

"Ay, calm yourself, bambino!"

"I'm sorry!" I released a harsh breath and scrubbed my hands over my face, then groaned and cursed and—fuck. I had to get my shit together. *Deep breaths, deep breaths.* I chewed on my thumbnail and put all my focus on not tapping my feet restlessly or drumming my fingers against the armrest.

Anthony maneuvered his truck through the Manhattan traffic like a pro, but I wished he'd slow down. He was driving me toward my fate way too quickly.

I hadn't been able to eat breakfast this morning. I'd fried up some eggs and bacon for my brother, and I'd almost hurled at the smell. That was how nervous I was. 'Cause I fucking loved bacon, otherwise.

This wasn't gonna go well. I could feel it.

All signs pointed to disaster.

Starting with the fact that today would be the absolute first time I saw Gideon in broad daylight. It felt so weird to even think about seeing him when the sun was out. Anthony had looked at me like I was crazy when I'd said this was a bad omen, but it was the little things, right? Gideon and I had never done anything normal. No dates, no lazy mornings in bed, no going out for coffee, no meeting up for lunch during our workdays, none of that. We'd been creatures of the night and of secrecy.

How was that a solid foundation to build a relationship on? Madonn'.

And then...and then, I didn't know his address! I didn't know where he lived! We'd had to spend a solid hour going through Gideon's Instagram for clues. He'd started the account in an attempt to get more information on me, yet he'd already posted 176 pictures of Chester. Three of them thankfully with a view of Central Park. In short, we'd managed to narrow down Gideon's address to two buildings, and he'd told me the night we went to that place with the delicious fries that he lived two streets away, so we were starting with that.

While my brother had gotten stuck on Gideon actually having a view of Central Park in his Upper East Side condo, I couldn't stop thinking about how I was ready to sign my life away to a man whose home I'd never visited.

And I fucking was. I was ready to spend the rest of my days with him. I loved him so much that it hurt.

I *missed* him, and I'd seen him last night. It was bonkers.

"Sometime today!" Anthony honked at the Civic ahead of us that was missing that the light had turned green, and when that didn't work, my brother rolled down the window and yelled. "Are you driving today, sunshine?" He honked some more. "Oi! Get off the fucking road!"

The asshole in front of us gestured for us to go around, so I guessed he was just gonna sit there on the corner and watch the day go by.

Anthony muttered a string of curses and drove around the fucker.

"I'm surprised you didn't flip him off too," I said in amusement.

"I'm not from Jersey. There are limits."

I let out a laugh, though it was short-lived. We were almost at the park.

"Let's see." He leaned forward and squinted at the street signs. "We should come up here..." He turned left, and I saw the trees straight ahead. Park Avenue was right up there, and if our guess was correct, the building to my right was Gideon's. "You got this, little brother."

I swallowed hard as he slowed down. There was no place to park.

I opened the door and stepped out into the cold Sunday morning.

He gave me a reassuring smile. "No matter what, we've got your back. I'll stay close until you call or text."

I nodded. "*Grazie.*" After closing the door, I took a deep breath and snuck between two parked cars and stepped onto the sidewalk. There was no strategy; I would just ask the doorman, or if there was a lobby, or...fuck if I knew. I'd been with clients in the past where it was like checking in to a hotel, and I'd been with clients where you went straight up.

As I rounded the building, I saw there was a doorman, at least.

At the sound of a dog barking, I threw a glance across the avenue, and I came to an abrupt stop. Maybe my heart thudded to a halt for a beat too. Gideon was coming out of the park with a floppy little fur ball, and he picked up Chester once they reached the crosswalk.

November was putting a rosy tint in Gideon's cheeks. His

159

hair was windblown, and he'd replaced his suit and coat with jeans and a shorter parka.

It was amazing to see him like this, carefree and smiling at his dog, but it also felt like I was intruding. Like this wasn't our time to see each other. This was his domain, at a time of day that had never belonged to us.

Gideon crossed the street with Chester in his arms, and I forced my legs to carry me forward.

I cleared my throat.

My pulse skyrocketed.

"Gideon," I managed to get out.

He whipped his head my way and could not look more surprised.

Fuck, I knew he didn't like surprises.

I had to make this quick without imposing. Maybe he had plans. He definitely had his routines.

"Can we talk for a minute?" I asked, approaching him carefully.

He furrowed his brow and set down Chester. "I apologize. I didn't expect..."

"I know you didn't." I gestured for us to stand closer to the building. The sidewalks up here didn't get very crowded, but he wasn't the only one out with his dog this morning. "I just had to talk to you. Sorry about the ambush."

He fidgeted with the end of the leash. "Is something wrong?"

You tell me.

I leaned my shoulder against the wall and cracked my knuckles absently. "I wouldn't say wrong... I just wanna get something off my chest before our time runs out." Jesus Christ, my nerves were shot. No time like the present, right? *Here goes everything.* "Pick me, Gideon."

His gaze snapped up and met mine, and I swallowed against the onslaught of emotions that resurfaced without warning.

Fuck, fuck, fuck.

"Choose me. Not her," I said. "I don't think we can fit into each other's worlds, but I think we can create something that's just ours. And...maybe I can't promise you a life of perfect stability—I know I can't—but I promise to always pay attention to what you need. I promise to be there." I had to swallow again, not to mention blink past the sting in my eyes. "That house and those family traditions could be ours—with kids we adopt or whatever. Or surrogacy? I don't know. All I know is that I want a future with you. I want us to be real. And I want there to be a seat for you at the table when we have Sunday dinners at Nonna's. Hell, Pop already invited you."

My bravery was fading fast, mostly because I couldn't read Gideon's expression for shit.

Was it too much? Fuck. I'd ambushed him and then overwhelmed him. Great start of something he had no reason to believe I could handle.

"I shoulda called before." I rubbed my forefinger and thumb over my eyes and cursed myself.

"It's almost ten thirty," he mumbled. "Ten thirty...ten thirty." His jaw ticked, and he screwed his eyes shut for a moment. "I need a pause button. I need to stay calm and proceed according to my plan."

His... His plan.

I felt the color drain from my face, and it was as if someone had just kicked me in the stomach.

"Please be at the apartment tonight," he told me. "I want to explain—"

"Gideon!"

No. No, fuck that noise. I looked over my shoulder and didn't know whether to laugh or cry. That had to be Claire.

She was coming out of a taxi, all blond hair and crystal-blue eyes and designer clothes.

As I faced Gideon again and felt nausea creeping up my throat, he took a small step closer, and the panic was clear in his eyes. They were pleading with me.

The sheer desperation made me toss my own pain out the window, and I said, "You don't have to explain anything, but I'll be there tonight." There was no erasing the dullness from my voice, though.

The clicking of heels approached and wrapped up my minute. Time to take a hike.

He was gonna proceed with his plan.

He was choosing her.

"I'm sorry," he said quietly, right before Claire reached us.

She eyed me curiously. "Hello."

Fuck my life. I dropped my stare to the catalogues in her arms and saw at least one bridal magazine.

I grinned and shook my head. It was the only thing I could do if I didn't wanna flip my shit right here on the sidewalk. But my heart fucking broke.

"Who's this, Gideon?"

I pushed off the wall and took a step back. "You know who I am." With that said, I gave Gideon a last glance before I trailed back toward the street where Anthony had dropped me off.

Then something stopped me.

Claire said Gideon's name with enough worry in her voice that I had to look back, and when I saw that he was about to lose it, it wasn't about me anymore whatsoever. I'd made a promise. More than that, I couldn't look the other way—not even if I wanted to. So I hurried back to him and kidnapped the prover-bial remote control.

"Come here. Let's get you inside." I handed over the leash to Claire and positioned myself in front of Gideon. "Listen to me."

He managed to make eye contact, but I could sense it wouldn't last long. His breaths were coming out quicker and quicker, and his features were contorted in pain.

"This is highly inappropriate," Claire hissed under her breath.

I ignored her. This was my doing, and I was going to fix it.

"Just follow me, Gideon." I kept a grip on his arms and started walking backward.

The doorman offered his assistance, and Claire said something to him. I couldn't make out the words, and it didn't matter.

"I'm not going anywhere, hon," I said quietly, hopefully so only he heard it. "You've got your pause button, okay? Right now, we're just gonna get you upstairs."

He screwed his eyes shut halfway through the lobby, but he didn't stop following me. Step by step, I got him closer to the elevator until we were inside it. Claire pushed the button for the top floor, and Chester butted his little head against Gideon's leg.

"I can't believe this," Claire said.

I cupped Gideon's cheek. "We're almost there."

"You have no right to be here," Claire added irritably. "You two were supposed to see each other discreetly."

"I'm not disagreeing with you, but your fit's gonna have to wait," I told her. "I'll leave once he feels better."

"I can take care of my own fiancé," she snapped.

Someone give me strength.

Gideon clutched at my arms the second the elevator dinged, announcing our arrival on the top floor, and Claire took the lead. I wasn't at all bitter and jealous about her having keys to his place. There were only two doors to choose from, and I remembered Gideon mentioning a Mrs. Nelson.

Claire opened the door, and I registered the bare minimum, wanting my focus on Gideon. And maybe there was a side of me that just didn't wanna see his place now that it was tainted. *She* had ruined it.

Actually, I had ruined everything.

"Where's his bedroom?" I asked, shrugging off my jacket and kicking off my shoes. They landed on the floor. Gideon's jacket was next. He'd told me that the thing he disliked most about the studio apartment was that there was no hallway to hang your coat and put away your shoes. He didn't like wearing those items indoors, so I assumed he didn't want to walk farther in those shoes either. I helped him take them off.

Claire looked as if she didn't want us to go near that particular room, but I hoped she'd realize it would've been beyond stupid to think…I didn't even know, that I'd take him in there now to bend him over for me? *Cazzo.* But down the hall she gestured. Surrounded by shiny hardwood floors, intricate moldings, art, and rich colors, I ushered Gideon toward an open door and saw a big bed in the middle of the room.

He'd fucked her here, hadn't he? Of course he had.

I did my best to swallow the jealousy, and I sat Gideon down on the edge of the bed and stepped between his legs.

"Breathe with me, baby," I murmured.

He nodded jerkily and struggled to suck in a longer, slower breath.

"We'll push that pause button," I repeated. "You set the pace. Everything can wait."

Including me, even if he only wanted to see me later to explain why he was going to marry Claire.

He wrapped his arms around my midsection and pressed his face to my chest.

"I'm so fucking sorry for showing up unannounced." I pressed my lips to his hair and breathed him in. For all I knew, I wouldn't get another chance. It almost made me wanna beg him to keep coming to the apartment for whatever little time we had left of our two months, as if we could pretend after this. As if I could stomach his nightly visits for another week, knowing full well that he'd made his decision.

Chester appeared at our feet and head-butted Gideon's leg, then stood up on his hind legs and clearly wanted to get on someone's lap.

"Want me to get him for you?" I asked.

Gideon sniffled and shook his head before he released me. He was breathing easier now. In mere minutes, I wouldn't have a reason to stay anymore. He was getting better.

He picked up Chester and hugged the little dog to him.

It hadn't occurred to me before that Chester was his emotional support animal. Even if it wasn't intentional, even if Chester hadn't been trained as a support dog, that was clearly his role, and he seemed to be doing a great job. He wagged his furry little tail and tried to jump up toward Gideon's face.

I could take a hint. Time for me to bounce.

"I'm gonna go." I combed my fingers through Gideon's hair, and he closed his eyes and took a deep breath. "I'll be there tonight, okay?"

He nodded once and exhaled unsteadily. "And you promise we p-pushed the pause button?"

"I promise." I leaned down and kissed him on the forehead. "You tick things off one at a time, and I'll wait. Don't rush on anyone's behalf."

"Thank you." He squeezed my hand briefly. "I think I can be there around eight or nine."

"All right, I'll wait."

On the way out, I picked up my jacket and put on my shoes, and I avoided Claire altogether. Then I texted Anthony in the elevator, and by the time I reached the ground floor, he told me he would be outside the entrance in a minute.

Mannaggia, I couldn't believe myself. Too many emotions

were surging within me, and I couldn't shake the nausea. The only thing I knew for certain was that I'd screwed up royally.

My chest hurt. It hurt to breathe. It hurt to think.

Anthony rolled up in his black truck, and I met his cautious expression when I jumped in and slammed the door shut.

"I made a complete fool of myself."

I wanted to throw up.

He winced and pulled away from the curb. "Tell me what happened."

"Nicky. You can't lie here all day."

"Watch me," I mumbled around a spoonful of ice cream. Once we'd gotten back to the apartment, I'd showered, changed into sweats and a tee, created the biggest ice cream sundae for myself, then thrown myself onto the bed with my phone. And I wasn't going nowheres.

Maybe I'd stay here until Gideon's pillow stopped smelling like him.

Anthony sighed and sat down at my keyboard but turned the chair so he could face me.

"You don't gotta babysit me," I said. I kinda wanted to be alone, because I had an itch to go through my pictures. I had three of Gideon and two of him and me, silly and sweet selfies from our walks—okay, one of them was of the dirty variety. He'd taken the photo with my phone when I was blowing him. But all I wanted right now were the silly-sweet pics.

Anthony checked his watch. "Ruby will be here in an hour."

"And she will be about as entertained as you are now." I punched the pillows behind me into comfortable perfection, then leaned back with my ice cream and my phone. Legs criss-crossed under the covers, ice cream bowl on my lap. "Listen. I can't even tell you how thankful I am for you—and Ruby—but I'm gonna host this pity party with or without you. That includes ice cream, playing my game on my phone, and probably inhaling Gideon's scent on the pillows."

He smiled ruefully. "You know there's still a chance, bambino."

"Please don't." I shook my head and started a new level on my game. "I might need you tomorrow instead. Today I'mma wallow in despair."

I'd thought it would come out as a half-assed joke, but it fucking hurt.

"I'll leave you be and call off Ruby—on one condition," he said. "You come to my place tonight if things don't go well with Gideon. I can pick you up."

I nodded, agreeing, because that was already my plan. And if he was bringing his truck, I might as well bring all my shit. There wasn't a chance in hell I could stay here another night.

"I'll call you," I promised.

"*Bene.*" He rose from his seat and patted my knee. "I'll be at Pop's for a while. He needs help fixing the radiator in his bedroom, but I'll keep my phone close."

"You can fix radiators, but you can't make noodles," I mumbled, swiping a raspberry over a tomato on the screen.

Anthony laughed on his way out.

Gideon, that fucking bastard.

I sniffled and wiped at my cheek, and I couldn't even be happy about beating a really difficult level in my game, 'cause all I had in my head was something *he* had put there. The idea of having children.

I couldn't stop picturing it.

Before—never. Hadn't entered my mind. Or, I mean, something for "way down the road." Since there were so many obstacles before it became relevant. I needed a steady job, a home, solid income—and preferably a partner. Now I'd gotten the slightest glimpse of what that life could be like.

Gideon would make a good father.

He and I would make a great team. We had such different qualities, and combined...yeah. We'd nail that shit.

Maybe we'd have a boy and a girl? Or two brothers and a sister?

I sighed heavily and tossed my phone next to me. The grief rolled over me as I pulled the duvet higher, and I got weepy again because I couldn't sniff the pillow when my nose was stuffy.

The embarrassment from earlier today decided to come back too.

I'd been an idiot. Showing up unannounced was annoying to most people; he didn't have to be autistic for that. But to him... Christ. The slightest surprise turned into an ambush. And there I'd been, talking about how I'd pay attention to his needs?

I was a joke.

My stomach snarled with hunger, and I ignored it. I'd had three bowls of ice cream. That was enough. I'd racked up an impressive stack of dishes on the nightstand.

Tonight I'd be back in Anthony's guest room. Later tonight. Technically, it was already night. A glance at the alarm clock told me it was four minutes past seven.

Perhaps I hadn't matured as much these past two years as I wanted to believe. After quitting with Tina last time, I'd given myself a big ass-kicking for blowing through the money I'd earned while working for her. Granted, it meant I had one sweet fucking collection of instruments now, but that meant fuck-all when I had to crash with my brother.

While I'd saved most of the money from Gideon, I'd shown my immaturity in other ways.

My phone buzzed with a message, and I saw Gideon's name on the display.

Can I come now instead, please? I've calmed down sufficiently, and I need to see you.

I sniffled and typed in a response.

Yeah, sure.

I estimated that would give me approximately fifteen minutes to compose mys—

Two firm knocks on the door interrupted my thought.

Are you kidding me?

No, it could be Ruby. Maybe. For some reason. Plus, Gideon had a key.

I threw off the covers and grabbed as many wadded-up tissues as I could, and I threw them under the sink on my way to the door. My heart slowly but surely crept up in my throat, only for it to get lodged when I saw Gideon through the peephole. He was already here. And he wasn't dressed for success. He was wearing Yankee sweats and a hoodie.

I opened the door, figuring I was gonna do this without Instagram filters and fake smiles. I couldn't pretend, and there was no time to try to look like I hadn't wept like a baby earlier anyway.

He looked about as tired as I felt, and he frowned when his gaze landed on my face.

"I know, I look like shit." I opened the door wider and let him in.

He shook his head and stopped near the kitchen table. He was scanning the place for changes.

I locked the door again and returned to the bed. "Claire

busy picking out a wedding dress?" Ouch, too bitter. Well, there was no taking backsies, but I was keeping my mouth shut now. After pulling up the covers, I pulled up my knees too and hugged them to my chest.

Gideon was still frowning. "I highly doubt that considering I broke off our engagement—and she swiftly terminated our friendship as well."

I felt my forehead crease with confusion.

He did what?

The words didn't really compute.

"But you chose her," I said.

More frowning. At least he left the kitchen and moved closer. "Excuse me? I did no such thing."

My heart stayed in my throat, for a whole new reason, and it started beating furiously. "You said—I heard you, Gideon. You said you had to proceed with your plan. Your plan to marry her —it was your plan all along."

He stared at me as if he were trying to solve a difficult math problem, all while I went to war against the hope that threatened to shoot out of me. If there was the slightest chance...

"You're mistaken." He sat down on the edge of the bed and pulled up one of his legs so he could face me properly. "I was a nervous wreck all morning because I had invited Claire over to tell her I could no longer go through with the engagement. Then I took a walk with Chester to center myself, and when I came back, I saw you standing there. It threw me. It wasn't part of my plan."

I blinked. The words slithered through my brain too slowly, as if a part of me was scared shitless to believe them.

"It became too much, Nicky. With your declaration and Claire due to arrive at any moment, it was more than I could handle." He swallowed and stared at his lap. "You were also saying all the right things before I'd had the chance to admit the worst things about myself. So, I...I couldn't stave off the panic. And then she showed up, and I saw the magazines she was carrying." He blew out a breath and scrubbed his hands over his face. "She'd misunderstood me too. She'd thought I'd ended my 'experiment' with you early—and that I was ready to plan our wedding."

That was why he had asked for the pause button...

He hadn't been able to handle everything at once, so he'd told me he needed to stick to the plan—which was, end things with Claire, and *then* he and I could talk.

My eyes filled with unshed tears quicker than I could've anticipated, and I pressed my lips together to keep from making any weird sounds.

"I don't understand your emotions now," he stated.

"Relief." I blinked, and a couple tears fell down. "Plain relief."

I had a shot. It was official. I'd wear him down if I had to.

"Oh." He furrowed his brow. "I'm not there yet. I fear what I'm about to tell you will make you change your mind."

Unless he was hiding another fiancée somewhere, I wasn't too worried.

"I'm listening." I wiped at my cheeks and took a steadying breath. "Just...scoot closer to me, okay?"

He scooted a little closer, though not enough for us to be able to touch each other, so I extended my hand, and he scooted a bit more. It was an improvement at least—and a much-needed comfort since he looked anything but at ease. In fact, his expression was pinched with worry and weariness.

I covered his hand with mine and gave it a squeeze. "Whatever it is you gotta tell me, it can't be that bad."

"You don't know that," he responded quietly. "We can start with today. I'm not good at communicating properly at all times."

"Who is?"

He huffed a breath. "Fine. I'm afraid I will bore you. I don't mind going to bars every now and then, but I can't stay very long, and I don't enjoy nightclubs at all. I'm also picky about restaurants, I'm not flexible, sometimes I might become clingy and needy—especially where you're concerned—and I'm positively terrified that your family won't accept me, and I know how much you love them." He hauled in a breath and trucked on. "Occasionally, I will avoid an issue and hope it goes away by itself. Most recently, it's been the matter of us not having sex."

This, I had to hear.

"When I have a lot on my mind..." he said, faltering, and he avoided eye contact more than before. Now he was almost peering toward the kitchen. It was clear he struggled with this. He was embarrassed. "I go through asexual periods sometimes."

Oh.

"I can't explain it very well." He wrung his hands awkwardly in his lap. "I can still feel incredibly affectionate toward you and want to please you, but I'm starting to believe it's because of my emotional attachment. It isn't sex. Not in the past few days anyway. That urge...disappears. Thankfully not for long, usually—perhaps a couple weeks or so—but it happens. I'm sorry."

Not a single thing he'd said raised any worries until those last two words. I wouldn't have him apologizing for shit.

Summoning my balls, I crawled over to him and climbed onto his lap.

"Hey." I kissed his forehead and decided not to force eye contact. He'd get there when he was ready, just like he had the first time we'd been in this position and I'd taken off my blindfold. "Don't apologize for who you are, papito."

"It's still a nuisance."

"Not really. It *is* understandable, though." I gathered his hands in mine and kissed his knuckles. "These past two months have turned both our worlds upside down. It'd be weird if that sort of exhaustion didn't manifest itself somehow."

He glanced down at our joined hands, and I decided to rewind the tapes and tackle the rest of what he'd said.

"My family will adore you and show you in their special way," I murmured. "I'll be your translator, and I'll give you all the heads-ups you might need. For instance, my nonna will try to force-feed you, because she thinks everyone under three hundred pounds is skinny, and you won't be able to say no to her."

His mouth twitched a little.

"I'll talk to her too." I bumped my forehead gently against his. "And let's make one thing clear. The first and the second, maybe even the third time you and I go over to hers for dinner, we'll both be nervous. You'll worry about stepping on any toes and saying the wrong thing, and I'll worry about not being able to calm you down enough. But at the end of the day, if my family sees that I'm happy, they're happy." What was next? Oh, the social life crap. "Now. Going out on the weekends and whatever. You're obviously gonna meet Ruby and Chris, and I'll be stoked whenever you come with us to a bar. But I will totally understand when you don't feel up to it—hell, sometimes I don't either. It's unfair to compare how often I go out when I'm single to how I wanna spend my time with you. I'm not as social as you think."

He cleared his throat and raised a brow, and the seconds-long look he gave me made me grin.

"Fine, by your standards, maybe I am social," I chuckled. "My point is, I love staying at home. It's what I prefer. I wanna have movie nights and make dinner together and just be with you." I eased the pad of my thumb over the worry lines between his eyebrows. "We also never stay out very long, my friends and

I. We're busy with our own lives. Most of the time, it's a couple drinks, and then someone's yawning because they've had a long day."

Some of the tension left his shoulders, and he leaned forward to drop his forehead to my shoulder.

"I already know you're picky and not flexible." I kissed the side of his head. "I'm the opposite, so chances are I won't fight you if you have a strong preference. And sometimes we'll compromise. Sometimes I'll push. We'll talk, we'll make mistakes, we'll even fight, but as long as we have each other's backs and wanna be together, we'll work things out."

He hummed. "You make it sound easy. I hate embarrassing myself, not to mention others. What if I embarrass *you*? I need breaks sometimes, you know. If it's too loud in a restaurant, I excuse myself to go to the bathroom, but...and please don't take offense, but if the display between you and your father after the concert is any indication of what a Sunday dinner is like, what if —I mean—how—" He cursed and stumbled over his words.

"Hey. Look at me, honey." I cupped his cheeks and got him to stop hiding against my neck. "First of all, it's impossible to embarrass me. Second of all, I want us to be a team. If it's that important to you to be discreet about wanting a breather, we'll come up with a system. You can signal to me whenever you need to duck out for a moment, and we'll take turns coming up with excuses. Maybe I'll send you down to the car to get something, or maybe you can step outside with Anthony when he takes a smoke. Or, if you want Nonna to fuss over you and give you extra dessert, you pretend to take a work call in the stairway, and when you come back, she'll express her worry about you working too much by filling your plate."

There were countless options. It wasn't an issue.

It seemed to be a big deal to Gideon, however. His eyes

became misty, and he managed a wobbly smile. "You'd do that for me?"

"Of *course*." I rested my forehead against his and wiped my fingers under his eyes. "Just be patient with me. I fucked up badly today, and I need time to learn your cues and recognize your needs better. I shouldn't have just shown up like that."

He shook his head and closed his eyes as he drew in a deep breath. "You don't understand the impact you've had on me. I feel more alive now than I ever have, and I welcome the moments of discomfort if it means I'm making strides forward with you. For goodness' sake, you give me memories worth remembering." When he opened his eyes again, they were clearer and more beautiful than ever. There was a spark of hunger, of determination. "I foolishly thought you'd be another temporary obsession at first, but I could not have been more wrong."

Oof, serious case of nerves suddenly wreaked havoc in my stomach.

He inched back slightly and didn't waver. "I don't know the exact moment I chose you, Nicky, but I knew there was no going back when I saw you with that little girl at the recital. She sat on your lap and gave you the biggest hug when her mother showed up." He paused. "I practiced those words on the way over here."

I grinned widely and became all mushy again.

We were fucking happening.

"Good emotions?" he asked, to make sure.

I nodded and wrapped my arms around his shoulders. "Overwhelmingly good. A future with you is all I want."

His expression softened. "Me too." Then he leaned in and kissed me gently, and it was the perfect way to continue after our tumultuous beginning. I wanted heaps of comfort. My body screamed to be held and, fuck, I wanted to *sleep*. Believing I'd lost the man of my dreams for even a day had drained me completely.

"Let's get under the covers," I mumbled against his lips. "I wanna make out and cuddle. And sleep without setting the alarm for dawn."

Because we finally had longer than that.

"Sounds perfect to me." He grasped the bottom of my tee and pulled it over my head. "I missed you."

God. Those words...

"I missed you too."

EPILOGUE

A FEW HOURS LATER

I woke up in the middle of the night when I heard rustling beside me. It sounded like I did when I tore out lyrics from my notebook in frustration.

Squinting at Gideon, who was more of a black silhouette in front of the lamp on the nightstand, I saw he was jotting something down on a notepad.

"Papi, get back to sleep…"

"In a moment." He raked his teeth over his bottom lip and kept writing. "Sorry if I woke you."

"It's okay. What're you doing?" I yawned and stretched out next to him.

"Making lists," he replied. "I don't want to miss any important steps in our relationship."

I grinned sleepily and hugged his thigh under the duvet, and I brushed my hand over his cock.

"I've also narrowed it down to two terms of endearment I'd like to use for you," he added.

"Oh yeah? What are they?" I dropped a kiss to his thigh as I stroked his cock absently. He was a shower and had a fairly large dick even when he was soft, and I wanted it in my mouth but figured he was busy doing his thing now. It was possible I had a one-track mind, but in my defense, he'd spoiled me with a shit-load of sex. He was the one who'd made me obsessed with his body.

"You know I'm not going to get hard, right?" he asked carefully.

"Yeah—and? Your cock is snuggly."

He snorted and relaxed. "By the way, you have a couple text messages."

I hummed. They were probably from Anthony and Ruby. I'd texted them both before we crashed last night.

"The terms of endearment," I reminded.

"Right. Question. Can I also call you baby, or is that taken? Because I like it, especially when we're in bed."

He could definitely call me baby.

"It's not taken. I'll be your perfect baby boy whenever you want it." Needing more, I crawled under the covers and between his legs, where I sucked his cock into my mouth.

His breath hitched a little, and he set down the notepad. "You do look perfect when you suck on me." He wove his fingers into my hair and sighed contentedly. "I want to call you sweet-heart too. When you're sweet, anyway. Not when you're a desperate little slut."

Fuuuck.

Safe to say, I was getting hard fast.

"Do you want me to take care of you?" he murmured.

I nodded, and my body took over. Or the desperation did. "Yes, please."

"Okay. I want to try a toy on you. Lie on your back and spread your legs for me."

Yes, sir.

As I obeyed and got into position, I asked if he could tell me what else was on his lists. Because no matter how horny I was, I was more hooked on us finally being together, and I wanted to see if there was anything else that melted my damn heart. He had his way of doing that.

"It's mostly milestones and things I've wanted to do during these past two months that have been too...you know, relationship-themed." He was slipping into his role of frank, factual, and almost detached Dominant, and it was as sexy as ever. It was the combination of hot and cold that did it for me, the mixing of sweet, nurturing Daddy and impersonal filth.

"Like what?" I bit my lip and watched as he poured lube over the dildo I'd gotten that resembled his cock.

"Dates, for instance," he said. "I want to take you out for breakfast in the morning, if you don't mind. I've never been on a date like that, and I like breakfast. Breakfast is the coziest of meals. I picture us sitting close together and eating bagels and watching people walk by."

I smiled like the love-sick idiot I was. "It's a date."

He flashed me a quick smile in return but was full steam ahead mentally and had already moved on to the next topic. It was easily noticeable when he forgot to react to something.

"I've also been looking at real estate in Brooklyn," he said frankly. "Your brother chose well. Park Slope is lovely and has great schools."

He didn't understand the magnitude of what he was saying. To me, it was the most reassuring thing in the world. This was legit. He was serious about us. And Brooklyn? Fuck me twice, just that he was considering living there... I had no words for it. He could pick whatever neighborhood he wanted.

"You realize Park Slope has nothing I can afford, right?" I had to throw that out there.

He furrowed his brow and wiped his hand on a tissue. "I do realize that. It's on my list of things I'd like to have a veto on. Or rather, things I'd like to be in charge of completely."

This oughta be good…

"How long is this list?"

"Only three items, so far," he assured. "One, I don't want any money talk. The life you're giving me—and the life I want us to give each other—can't be quantified and price-tagged. I'd rather we toss all our strengths and weaknesses, assets and so on, and just mix it all together and call it ours." He paused and leveled me with a serious look. All while holding a lubed-up dildo in his hand. "I genuinely believe this will cause the least amount of arguments."

There would be *some* arguments about it, 'cause two months weren't enough to build a foundation on, in which I suddenly possessed half of his wealth. Life didn't work that way.

"We can negotiate the terms," I bargained, "but you can decide where we live when that day comes."

"I'd really prefer if you just agreed with me."

I let out a loud laugh and scratched my stomach. "I'm sure you would, papito. But that's not why you're dating me. As much as it'll frustrate you, you know I'll do the right thing and slow us down a little so we can enjoy dating properly, meeting up frequently and fucking our way through our most intense honeymoon phase, spoiling each other rotten with thoughtful little gifts, and texting too much how we miss each other when we're at work. No one's getting unnecessarily overwhelmed on my watch."

He opened his mouth to respond, only to close it again and smile softly. "I like that vision."

"So do I." I extended a hand to him, wanting him close, wanting…fuck. Everything. I had to let him know that I was serious too. Taking things slowly in the beginning was good, but that didn't mean I didn't want everything he'd talked about, including a home together and a good school district. "Come kiss me."

He grinned and crawled over to me, and I pushed myself up on my elbows and met him in a deep, languid kiss.

I didn't even know where he'd gotten the chocolate from this time, but he definitely tasted of it.

"I love you, Gideon."

He broke away from the kiss and flicked his gaze to meet mine.

I stroked his cheek.

"Are you certain?" he asked.

I chuckled. "I've never been more sure."

He kissed me again, harder this time, and it wasn't an awesome kiss, because he couldn't keep from smiling, which sort of made it the perfect kiss instead.

"I love you too," he said and backed away. "I didn't think you were there yet, but it's on the list." He reached for the nightstand and plopped down on his stomach, dildo still in hand, and he flipped through the pages of the notepad. "Now I can cross it off. That's always satisfying."

I rubbed a hand over my mouth and tried to withhold the laughter, but I fucking couldn't. He was too much sometimes, in the best ways; there was an innocence in his behavior that I loved more than anything. It was reassuring and comforting, to be honest. He wasn't the kind of man to play games or have hidden agendas.

But yeah, I'd totally lost my hard-on.

"Hon, I think we're gonna have to get dirty another time." I smirked and smacked him on his ass.

"Nonsense. I'll get you hard in a minute," he said dismissively, returning the notepad to the nightstand. "You just need some Daddy-time and a big cock."

I sucked in a breath.

Okay, that would work.

A FEW WEEKS LATER

I took a sip of my coffee and threw a cursory glance at Gideon's phone, and I couldn't believe it. I almost choked on my beverage.

"How the fuck have you passed me already?" I asked incredulously.

He raised a brow but never actually looked away from his screen. "Presumably because I'm better at this game than you are. It's very easy."

The man did not know how to sugarcoat.

He sniffled and kept playing, and I had to remind him to drink his coffee and eat his pastry. New York was covered in snow, and we'd taken shelter from the cold in a French pastry shop near Macy's. Gideon had just survived a four-day man cold and didn't need to get sick again. But since we were going to Nonna's for Thanksgiving tomorrow—his first time meeting my whole family—he'd insisted we go out and buy something to bring them.

"I struggled forever with that level." I side-eyed him and his damn phone.

"We all have our strengths and weaknesses, sweetheart."

I snorted and shook my head in amusement.

All banter aside, downloading that game had helped him immensely. It'd started with his curiosity when I had bitched at a difficult level, and I'd ended up asking him for help. He'd crushed it in two minutes and then started playing too. And he said it was a perfect distraction for when his mind was too chaotic. He'd also come home to the apartment one day, sheepish as hell, and admitted that he'd lost track of time at lunch and played in his office when he was supposed to have been in a meeting.

"Nailed it. Again." He shut his phone and pocketed it with a satisfied smile. "When is Anthony due?"

"Any minute, I guess." My brother had texted when he'd gotten on the subway. He was the one with the original errand at Macy's. Every Christmas, he gave Nonna her favorite perfume that could only be bought there, and he hated shopping closer to the holiday. He also didn't have the patience for online shopping, which was a dumb excuse for the fact that he was bad with computers.

Gideon had picked Macy's and asked me to ask Anthony if we could meet up for coffee.

My man wanted to make new friends, and he was so sweet about it. It was also possible he was still shell-shocked from meeting Ruby that he planned on latching on to the first option that wasn't as wild as... Well, I couldn't say it was just Ruby. It was more a combination of her and me together. Gideon was fascinated by her and found her "lovely," but he couldn't keep up.

Either way, Anthony was a perfect candidate.

"Can I try yours, please?" Gideon pointed his fork at my raspberry mousse pastry.

"It wasn't as sweet as I thought it would be." I slid the plate closer to him.

He made a grimace when he tried it. "No. Too tart."

I chuckled.

He held up a forkful of chocolate cake for me to try, and I closed my mouth around it.

"Damn." I chewed slowly, a bit overwhelmed by the sugar explosion. "Here, lemme try something." With a little bit of mine and a little bit of his on the same fork, I fed him the combination, and his eyes lit up in approval. "Yeah?"

He nodded. "Definitely."

"Oi, lovebirds." Anthony appeared between the tables, looking sufficiently frazzled after a ride on the subway to the borough he hated.

"Hey!" I grinned and kicked out his chair. "You ready for a day of shopping?"

He raised his brows and shrugged out of his jacket. "Day? I'll be in and out in ten minutes."

Kinda like Gideon this morning. He'd been feeling "too sick" to come with me for my walk, but joining me in the shower for a quickie was no problem. So, I had walked Chester, something I'd started doing the other week when we spent the night at Gideon's place the first time.

We were both in agreement that the studio was more for us; it was ours, in a sense, and he was ready to start fresh elsewhere. But when he had to work from home, I brought my ass up to the Upper East Side. Most of the time anyway. I spent the night at Anthony's quite a bit too, 'cause work was busy right before the break, with all the recitals and so on.

Anthony went up to the register and ordered coffee, and I leaned over and kissed Gideon's cheek.

"How are you feeling?"

"I'm okay. Anthony doesn't make me nervous."

That wasn't what I'd been referring to—I was thinking about his cold—but that was good. Our first "official" get-together had involved Anthony inviting us over for pizza and beer, and we'd ended up having a great time. We'd even spent the night there because we'd been buzzed.

"Neither will Pop and Nonna after tomorrow," I promised.

Because I'd had a chat with both of them. Nothing big, I just wanted to make sure they'd go easy on the nosiness.

Gideon squeezed my leg under the table. "To be honest, I'm not as worried anymore. If there's one thing I've learned lately, it's to focus on what matters. Your family is accepting, regardless of how boisterous they might be. I'll be fine."

Fuck. I slipped my hand into his and squeezed back. I knew he was bothered by his "coming out" to his family. Among those he worked with, it'd been an anticlimactic affair; his cousin's son —who Gideon referred to as a nephew—had even mentioned he'd suspected Gideon was gay. Or bi, in his case. But there'd been some "concerns" raised by other family members. The kind that went, "We support you no matter what. We're just worried about how this might affect your life." Then some self-appointed patriarch of the family had suggested that they "keep this development private."

I couldn't blame Gideon for never having felt close to them. They seemed frigid, the bunch of them. And fuck them. Most of them weren't even in direct line to the Grant fortune; they just acted superior with all their gold sticks shoved up their asses because they felt entitled.

"I love you." I brought his hand to my lips and kissed his fingers.

He smiled, and it reached his eyes, thank God. "I love you too. Please don't be worried, Nicky. I'm finally happy."

Good.

Anthony returned to the table with his coffee and a scone, not to mention a rant about how people in the city couldn't behave for shit. I didn't ask why. It was always some small thing. Like the other members of my family, Anthony would always find a reason to complain about Manhattan.

"Speaking of absolutely not that," I drawled, "Gideon has a question."

"Yeah?" Anthony faced Gideon and sipped from his coffee.

"Yes." Gideon cleared his throat. "I was wondering if you wouldn't mind helping me finding a Christmas present for Nicky."

Nothing like bonding over shopping for me...

I smiled around a forkful of cake.

"I don't mind. That one's easy to shop for," Anthony replied. "If you haven't noticed already, he tends to post pictures on Instagram of shit he wants. Kid can't spell subtle."

"And that's a good thing!" I insisted.

"I'm inclined to agree," Gideon chuckled.

Anthony shook his head in amusement at me before giving his attention to Gideon again. "We can meet up one day when he's got work," he said. "He works later than I do on Thursdays."

"Terrific. I appreciate it," Gideon said. Then he flicked me a hesitant look. "Was that why you posted a photo of that cast-iron skillet?"

I leaned over and kissed his cheek. "You catch on quick, papi. I wanna cook for you, and we'll need new shit when we move in together."

He loved it whenever I brought up us moving to Brooklyn, and I loved making plans for it. Other than instruments and the occasional clothing item, I didn't shop much. Now, suddenly, a whole new world had opened up. I was looking at inspiration online for kitchens and bathrooms and bedrooms and home offices—his demand—and home studios—my down-the-road wish.

I'd yet to venture into the universe of interior design for kids' rooms, 'cause I had a feeling I'd spend money prematurely. Maybe things we wouldn't end up needing. I already had family who did that. Pop's sister, for instance, who bought a bunch of pink stuff for her granddaughter who turned out to be a grandson.

"Do you know when you're moving yet?" Anthony asked around a mouthful of food. "I don't mean to rush you, but you know Nonna's gonna ask tomorrow."

I scratched my nose. "Well, we talked about it..." I glanced at Gideon, because he was in charge of all that.

"We're hiring a Realtor after the holidays," he said. "I'm doing my best to pace myself, but I'm not very good at it."

I laughed and kissed his shoulder. "You know I'm not-so-secretly thrilled that you're impatient, right?"

"I do, it's just frustrating that you're the mature one," he joked.

Anthony let out a laugh. "There's a first time for everything."

"*Ay.*" I flipped my fingers under my chin.

Anthony gave Gideon a "You see what I mean" look, and my man boarded the train to Mock Nicky Town.

I couldn't say I minded, though. It was a good way for them to grow closer as buddies.

A FEW MONTHS LATER

Gideon quickly learned the ropes around Nonna's house, and he discovered the way to their hearts was to be interested in Nonna's cooking and listen to Pop when he talked engines and cars. In a family full of loudmouths, a listener could go far doing nothing. 'Cause wasn't that what we loudmouths wanted? Someone to listen to us?

That said, I didn't expect Gideon to grow so close to my grandmother. Anthony? Definitely. And they did meet up from time to time to chat and watch old baseball games—while waiting for the next season—and they had a friendly rivalry going on, what with my brother rooting for the Mets and Gideon being a Yankees fan. But it was Nonna whom Gideon formed a special attachment to, and it was hella mutual.

In retrospect, it made more sense. Gideon had missed having a motherly type who fussed over him, and apparently Nonna loved having someone around who wasn't just there to fill their stomach. Anthony and I were bad, bad grandsons.

"When are youse leavin'?" Pop asked, never taking his eyes off the TV.

"Still three weeks to go," Anthony replied patiently.

I was less patient. Pop had asked the same question the last four Sunday dinners. I guess it proved that we didn't leave New York very often, because us going to Nashville next month was a huge deal to Pop.

"Nicky, get me another beer, will ya?"

"Yes, sir." I got off the couch and trailed into the kitchen where Nonna and Gideon were finishing up the preparations for dinner. Okay, Nonna cooked, and Gideon listened to her talking about...something.

"Try this, *tesoro*." Nonna held up a spoon. A regular spoon. At some point, she must've found out that Gideon was uncomfortable tasting from the wooden spoon used for stirring.

"Oh, that's delicious." Gideon wiped his mouth. "Best marinara I've ever tasted."

"You're so sweet!"

I shook my head, more than a little insulted. "Nonna, he gets to sample, and I don't?"

"Pshh-taa!" She completely waved me off. "He helped me buy the ingredients earlier this week. Were you there? Huh? I don't think so!"

I mock-scowled at Gideon, who looked way too smug, and then I opened the fridge to grab another can of beer.

Dinner smelled amazing. I was so hungry. Practically starving. Gideon and I had been to four freaking open houses today, and nada. I'd thought they were all beautiful houses, but Gideon, man...so goddamn picky. It had to be perfect. And when he listed his reasons, it was impossible to be annoyed with him. Big kitchen so we could cook together and host dinners, rooms for future children, a master bedroom close to aforementioned future children's rooms, preferably close to a good school too, there had to be some type of yard...

At this rate, we were never finding a place.

"Where were we?" Nonna mused. "Oh! Right, you were wondering about staying at home. So, I gave up my job, and you know—best decision I ever made. I got to watch my babies grow up. That's time you can never get back."

I paused in the doorway and wondered why they were talking about such a thing. Was Gideon thinking about being a stay-at-home dad? He'd mentioned being willing to walk away from it all before...

"And Frank—God rest his soul—" Nonna made the Sign of the Cross, referring to my grandfather, who died years ago "—he worked hard for us. Never complained."

Funny how dead people became saints. Nonno had been a funny old dude who'd once taught me how to cheat at street craps, and he used to sneak beers to Anthony—oh, and one more thing. He'd loved to complain!

I lifted a brow at Gideon.

Nonna was still rambling, so Gideon smiled faintly and shook his head at me, indicating he'd tell me later.

Fine. Just ignore me, then!

I went back to the living room and handed Pop his beer.

"We've been replaced, haven't we?" Anthony asked.

"Yup." I sat down with a sigh. "I'm a little jealous."

Pop laughed gruffly. "You poor schmucks."

"Uh, *yeah.*" I widened my eyes at him.

"Bah!" He waved me off too. Great.

I rolled my eyes and folded my arms over my chest. I supposed there was nothing to do but watch the goddamn Weather Channel with Pop and Anthony while Gideon got to try the marinara and the meatballs and maybe even dessert. She was making her lemon ricotta crostata with cherry sauce today, and it was one of my favorites.

Bored, hungry, and a little moody, I leaned back and let my eyes wander. Nonna's apartment hadn't changed much in the last two or three decades, from the floral patterns on the wallpaper and the lace tablecloth on the coffee table, to the yellowing pictures on the walls and the old TV. Much was homemade or hand-me-downs or stuff she'd bought at flea markets, and despite that, coming here was invaluable to me. Even more so lately, because her home had always lived and breathed family, and it was something I wanted to capture in my future home with Gideon.

"I'm telling you," Pop exclaimed, "that storm's coming here. Mark my words! Maybe it'll flood again."

Anthony and I exchanged a look.

After Hurricane Sandy, Pop thought every rainstorm was gonna turn into a biblical event with its destruction. We felt a little bad for him, so we didn't say anything, but it was getting tedious. He was obsessed with checking the weather.

"*Mangia!*" Nonna finally hollered. "And I don't wanna find any empty cans and glasses in the parlor later!"

First real Italian word I'd taught Gideon. When he heard *mangia*, and he heard it a lot nowadays, it meant eat, eat, eat. All the eating.

Pop pushed mute on the TV, and we abandoned the living room with our sodas and beers.

We were met by a fresh waft of garlic from the bread coming outta the oven, and my stomach snarled with want.

This was what Sundays were all about.

Food and family.

A FEW YEARS LATER

I grinned and pinched my lips together, willing myself not to get mushy.

It was probably a good thing I wasn't in the rehearsal room, but no one could stop me from watching through the window. Anthony had already spotted me. His patience was out of this world, and he was making such progress with Hannah. She finally trusted him completely.

She bobbed her head unsteadily and tinkered on the little pink guitar, a gift from Anthony when she turned six earlier this year. Whenever he praised her, she became so excited she couldn't sit still. Maybe she didn't always express herself verbally, but the girl had no issues getting her message across anymore. She did talk a lot more now too.

Anthony smiled widely when she'd done something, and I wanted to be in there; I wanted to hear them.

The door opened next to me, and Gideon hurried in and removed his gloves. "Did I miss it?"

I shook my head and extended my hand. "She's doing so fucking well."

He grabbed it and peered through the window. Then he released a breath and looked like everything was right in the world.

And it was.

We'd started out as foster parents to a three-year-old who hadn't been diagnosed yet. She'd also never spoken a single word at that point. But Gideon had walked away from most of his responsibilities at the family corporation to stay at home with her, to connect with her, to tutor her, and we'd started building our family around us. Around Hannah.

"Good job, Hannah," I read on Anthony's lips, and she shimmied in her seat.

"Can we go in?" Gideon murmured.

"I was thinking we don't wanna distract her," I said, but I left it up to him. With Hannah, I let Gideon set the pace a bit more, 'cause he was so in tune with her needs.

"I think she'll be fine," he replied. "She's been doing better with her discipline exercises."

True, and definitely no need to twist my arm. I reached up and kissed his cheek, then opened the door to the rehearsal room, and Hannah's mouth popped open before her green eyes lit up.

"Daddies! I'm playing."

"That's amazing, baby girl," I praised. "Daddy and I are just gonna sit here and watch, okay? You concentrate on what Uncle Anthony's teaching you."

She nodded and put on her serious face as Gideon and I sat down in two of the chairs along the wall.

Gideon threaded our fingers together and didn't take his eyes off Hannah. "By the way, whatever it is you've got cooking in the Crock-Pot at home smells a little too good."

I chuckled silently and kissed his knuckles.

The clock on the wall struck six, and I asked him if we were picking up Sammy or if Ruby was bringing him over. My party-loving best friend was terrified because she was expecting her first child, so she'd volunteered to watch our hellion some afternoons.

I wasn't sure it would make her any less scared, to be honest.

"She's dropping him off here," Gideon replied quietly. "Apparently, Sam was a great little helper with the dishes."

I quirked a brow. "Actually helping or...did he throw plates on the floor again?"

With our toddler, you could never be certain.

"Actually helping," Gideon laughed softly.

Good. Sammy may not share my genes, but Pop liked to point out how our boy was as rambunctious as I had once been.

If Hannah and Gideon had their extra special bond, Sammy and I had ours. He loved sitting with me when I played whatever instrument, but he also required a firm hand that Gideon was less happy about providing. The husband was a sucker, in short.

I didn't mind. Before meeting Gideon, before having kids with him, I'd never thought I would find my dream in the very moment I came home from work, kissed a tired Gideon hello, got an update on everything, then spent some time laying down the law to our son because Gideon hadn't been able to. I just fucking lived for it. Then I'd make us dinner while my man got some rest, and we'd eat together and swap stories about our day. Starting next year, it would involve homework for Hannah, which was nuts. She was growing up too fast.

Part of me wanted one more—three was a good number. Another part of me really fucking enjoyed arranging for babysitters within the family so Gideon and I could fuck off for a weekend here and there.

Maybe when Sammy got a little older.

Either way, I was ready for whatever life might throw at us, as long as we maintained our tradition of stopping for fries at

Gideon's favorite place on Saturdays. Otherwise, he got crankier than Sammy on an empty stomach.

But for now, we were going to sit here and feel ridiculously proud as our daughter played "Twinkle, Twinkle, Little Star" on her very own guitar.

Nicky and Gideon will be back in Anthony's story, We Have Till Monday, where the gang is off to Nashville.

MORE FROM CARA

Cara freely admits she's addicted to revisiting the men and women who yammer in her head, and several of her characters cross over in other titles. If you enjoyed this book, you might like the following.

We Have Till Monday
Daddykink | Vacation Romance | Regression Play | Age Difference | Rockstar Romance

When it seemed like everyone around Anthony Fender was reaching a goal or falling in love, he blamed an early midlife crisis for throwing him far outside of his comfort zone, all the way to Nashville. Hopefully, this vacation would bring him back to life—starting with a cooking class hosted by celebrity chef August King. But meeting the chef and his much younger husband Camden Adair changed everything. Their dynamic grabbed hold of Anthony and reeled him in before he even heard the magic word.

"Daddy."

Home
MM | Hurt/Comfort | Family Romance | Autism | Single Dad | Standalone

The day I stepped off the bus in Seattle, I hoped with every fiber of my being that my Philadelphia past was left behind me. I couldn't guarantee I'd be off the streets yet—far from it—but at least I'd see my little girl again. Then I met him. Adrian. A straitlaced history teacher. According to his brother, Adrian had a habit of rescuing strays, but I didn't buy the nice-guy act. Well, at first.

Top Priority
MM | The Game Series, #1 | BDSM | Daddykink | Standalone

In a perfect world, Lucas West would meet the Little he's fantasized about, and so would Colt Carter after he'd retired from the Air Force. In reality, the two Daddy Doms met each other. While waiting out a storm, there was only one way to tackle the chemistry between them, even though they both agreed it was a horrible idea.

Power Play
MM | Daddykink Romance | Age Difference | Mental Health | Standalone

Love sucked. Correction: it sucked when you were in love with your parents' closest friend and he didn't feel the same. Madigan had always been there for me, from when I was a kid to when I got drafted by the NHL. Then I made the mistake of confessing my feelings for him... I was such a loser. My bipolar disorder was already difficult to manage as it was; add high anxiety and, most recently, as the cherry on a shit sundae, a suspension from the team. Why couldn't he see that I was perfect for him? We even had kink in common! Not that he knew that...

The Guy in the Window
MM | Mild Kink | Age Difference | Taboo | Standalone

I was in the middle of my divorce when Adam messaged me. I believe his exact words were, "Hi. I think you're my dad's brother. Would you like to get to know me?" My brother and I had never been close, so I'd only met his adopted son a few times when he was very young. First, he became sort-of-my-nephew. Then he became the guy who helped me find an apartment, coincidentally across the alley from his own place. Then one night, as I got ready for bed, he became the guy in the window.

Check out Cara's entire collection at www.caradeewrites.com, and don't forget to sign up for her newsletter so you don't miss any new releases, updates on book signings, free outtakes, giveaways, and much more.

ABOUT CARA

I'm often awkwardly silent or, if the topic interests me, a chronic rambler. In other words, I can discuss writing forever and ever. Fiction, in particular. The love story—while a huge draw and constantly present—is secondary for me, because there's so much more to writing romance fiction than just making two (or more) people fall in love and have hot sex.

There's a world to build, characters to develop, interests to create, and a topic or two to research thoroughly.

Every book is a challenge for me, an opportunity to learn something new, and a puzzle to piece together. I want my characters to come to life, and the only way I know to do that is to give them substance—passions, history, goals, quirks, and strong opinions—and to let them evolve.

I want my men and women to be relatable. That means allowing room for everyday problems and, for lack of a better word, flaws. My characters will never be perfect.

Wait...this was supposed to be about me, not my writing.

I'm a writey person who loves to write. Always wanderlusting, twitterpating, kinking, cooking, baking, and geeking. There's time for hockey and family, too. But mostly, I just love to write.

~Cara.

Get social with Cara
www.caradeewrites.com
www.camassiacove.com
Facebook: @caradeewrites
Twitter: @caradeewrites
Instagram: @caradeewrites

Printed in Great Britain
by Amazon